HOME DETENTION

the making of a baby

by Michael Bent

First Published 2019

Copyright © AB Discovery 2019

All rights reserved.

Title: Home Detention

Author: Michael Bent

Editor: Rosalie Bent

Publisher: AB Discovery

© 2019

www.abdiscovery.com.au

Other Books from Michael and Rosalie Bent

There's still a baby in my bed!
So, Your teenager is wearing diapers!
Where Big Babies Live
Home Detention
Adult Babies: Psychology and Practices
Coffee with Rosie
Being an Adult Baby
The Three Chambers

Other Books from AB Discovery

A Brother for Samantha
Mommy's Diary
The Hypnotist
Chosen
The Snoop
The Washing Line
My Baby Callum
A Baby for Felicity
The Regression of Baby Noah
A Baby for Melissa and her Mother
Baby Solutions
Discharged into Infancy

The Bedwetter's Travel Guide
Me, Myself, Christine
Adult Babies: Psychology and Practices
The Joy of Bedwetting
Diaper Discipline and Dominance
Coffee with Rosie
Being an Adult Baby
The Adult Baby Identity – coming out as ABDL
The Adult Baby Identity – Healing Childhood Wounds

The English Baby

A Mother's Love

The Psychiatrist and her Patient

The Reluctant Baby

There's still a baby in my bed!

So, Your teenager is wearing diapers!

Where Big Babies Live

Home Detention

The Book Club Baby

The Rehab Regression

The Daycare Regression

The Virtual Reality Regression

A Woman's Guide to Babying Her Partner

The ABC of Baby Women

Overlapping Stains

The Babies and Bedwetters of Baker St

My Secret Needs and Desires

The Sissy Baby Nursery

Bedtime Stories for Sissy Babies (vol 1-3)

Living with Chrissie – my life as an Adult Baby

The Adult Baby Identity – a self-help guide

The Adult Baby Identity – the dissociation spectrum

Six Misfits

Six Misfits – A man and his dog

The Six Misfits – the seventh misfit

Becoming Me – The Journey of Self-acceptance

The Epitome of Love

Australian Baby: a life of diapers, bottles and struggles

Fear and Joy: a life in and out of diapers

The Fulltime, Permanent Adult Infant

Sissy babies: the ultimate submissive

Tales From The Nursery 1-6

The Better Husband Training Program

Max, the Diapered Zombie Killer

Living Happily as an Adult Baby

Belle Means Beautiful

Contents

Judgement

"Will the defendant please stand?"

Jordan Airesdale slowly stood up. His new suit, bought just for court, was uncomfortable, not that being in court facing sentencing was ever like to be anything other than very uncomfortable.

"You have pleaded guilty to breaking and entering, wilful damage and theft," the Magistrate continued. "Your partner has already been sentenced to jail and it is now my duty to sentence you to an appropriate period of detention."

Jordan's blood went cold. He had hoped to escape jail. He had turned eighteen only weeks earlier and could now be sent to an adult prison rather than a juvenile facility.

"The court has taken into account that you were not the ring-leader, but rather, the easily-led accomplice. Your criminal record to this point has been spotless, but your crime was significant and there was a large financial loss to the victims as well as psychological injury. If you had not pleaded guilty and not shown the remorse that you have done, this court would have had no other option than to send you to prison. But at the same time, the nature and outcome of your crime means that I cannot, therefore, let you off without *some* sentence of detention."

Jordan's lawyer grabbed his client's arm as he began to sway, looking as if he were about to collapse.

"However, the psychiatric report has indicated that you would suffer increased risks in prison and therefore, I am sentencing you to one year of home detention."

Jordan's heart began to beat again.

Home detention! I can do that!

"But understand this, Mister Airesdale. This means that you are to remain inside the boundary of your mother's home or any place that she moves to. You will be allowed to leave only to visit your probation officer, church and emergency medical needs. If at any other time you are found to be away from the home, you will immediately be arrested and taken to prison to serve the rest of your sentence. Do you understand?"

"Yes, Your Honour," he replied in a crackly voice.

"And if you come back to this court, your medical issues will not keep you away from prison a second time. You have been given one chance, young man. Don't waste it."

The making of a baby

The Magistrate stood up and the entire court did the same. Jordan turned around, still ashen-faced and saw his mother and older sister coming toward him. Neither was smiling.

"Let's get you home now," said Mrs Claire Airesdale icily. "You have disgraced us and our family name. Now you can spend the next year stuck inside."

His sister gave him an equally harsh look.

"But I am glad you won't be in prison," she added, showing just the hint of a smile. "And you can thank Doctor Woods for that."

Jordan knew that her mother and sister were very angry at him and with good reason. He had kicked himself repeatedly in the last six months for being so gullible and foolish as to follow Travis Morton, thug, criminal, and general waste-of-space. He had joined him on a burglary that had gone wrong and they were arrested within the hour. He only wanted a bit of excitement and he had certainly had that, but it was all the wrong kind of excitement. Since then, he had been terrified of going to prison.

Jordan was seventeen when he committed the crime, but had turned eighteen just before the trial. He pleaded guilty and had shown genuine remorse to the court. The elderly couple whose home they had burgled had, however, been traumatised to a great extent and had been forced to move to a nursing home. The Victim Impact Statement had been a devastating condemnation of his actions.

He was genuinely sorry and remorseful and he wanted to make amends, but for now, he was to spend the next year within the confines of his mother's smallish home in the inner city. The house was well presented and tastefully decorated in line with his family's modest wealth and position. But it had almost no back or front yard and he was already imagining spending an entire year trapped indoors with a mere fifty square metres of outside area to go to.

But anything is better than prison!

He consoled himself with that message and prepared himself for the difficulties to come.

The young man followed the court official into a side room to sign his release papers and to once again be informed of the onerous conditions of his home detention. He would not have to wear an ankle monitor as he had seen in countless American crime shows. But there would be random visits – day or night - and if he were not at home when they occurred... Prison.

He smiled as he walked out of the room after being told he was allowed to attend Church for ninety minutes once a week. That curiously Anglo-Saxon doctrine of not denying someone the right to worship had given him the chance of a weekly leave from his confines to go to Church. He had never gone in the past and yet now, the idea of a boring sermon and antiquated music was attractive compared to the confines of a home with his dominating mother and critical older sister.

"Come with me, Jordan," said his mother crisply. "You have to go home right now, so let's be off."

Claire slid into the driver's seat of her dark grey Jaguar XJ limousine. His sister, Connie, full name Constance Eileen Airesdale, slid into the passenger front seat while Jordan was once again, relegated to the rear.

He was the youngest child and the smallest and often felt like he was a disappointment. Certainly, the events of the day had not exactly disproven that assessment.

The Airesdales were that classic Family of Name that once possessed power, prestige, and influence, but now just had wealth – and modest wealth at that. Generations of indolence and waste had led to the family being relegated to one of historical significance, but contemporary irrelevance. Claire had been widowed five years before and at just forty-six years of age had used all the little influence she still had, to garner a reduced sentence for her son.

The making of a baby

Doctor Woods, Jordan's psychiatrist, had made a very positive and generous assessment of him to the court, despite some of his obvious flaws and character weaknesses. Jordan had a history of petty theft although none of it had been reported. He had been suspended twice from school and threatened with expulsion. Despite a first-class mind, he had failed to pass high school.

One of Claire's still influential contacts, someone who had once been a friend, passed on some 'advice' to the Magistrate to be lenient on him.

Claire had used up all of her influence and favours to keep her son out of prison. From now on, she was on her own. For all her hardness and feelings of loss, both of her husband and her position, she loved Jordan deeply. He was her only son and for all his flaws, she loved him and wanted desperately to protect him.

There had been one fact that she knew had tipped the balance between prison and home detention. One deep dark secret that Jordan did not want anyone to know, not even his doctor. But Claire had told his doctor about it regardless and was aware that the report she produced contained that secret in it. The doctor had shown her a copy beforehand, despite it being unethical to do so. Jordan did not know his mother had passed the secret on to the Doctor.

But it had worked in his favour. While all Claire's influence had managed to get his likely sentence reduced to less than a year in prison, this final secret was enough to move him from jail to home detention. The secret was immensely embarrassing.

Jordan Airesdale was a bedwetter.

And not just once a week with a small puddle. From the age of thirteen, after the death of his father, he had wet his bed every night, solidly and extensively. He had only been dry for barely a year before that devastating event, and the trauma of the death had triggered its return. And it had returned with a vengeance.

A heavy bedwetter in prison would have been tormented or worse and it was the key issue that had kept him from living behind

bars. It was the 'medical condition' that the Magistrate had so cryptically referred to.

Jordan knew none of this. Only his mother knew that her influence and her candour had saved him. And of course, his wet sheets.

Barnsdale

J ordan looked out the window of the car.

"Where are we going?" exclaimed Jordan, his voice rising in fear, as they left the courthouse. "This isn't the way home! If I don't get home in the next two hours, I will go to prison!"

"Stop worrying, convict," spat Connie, with a curious smile on her face.

The making of a baby

'Convict' was a new nickname and one he hoped wouldn't last. It was even worse than his normal nickname of 'stinky', a reference to his bedwetting.

"Connie is right, Jordan," explained his mother. "While you were busy getting yourself nearly in jail, I've bought all of us a new home out in the country."

"A new home?" spluttered Jordan. "You bought a new house and didn't even tell me? But I have to go to our old place!"

Jordan began to cry. It was one of his regular habits when upset and over the last few years, he would cry often. It was deeply embarrassing for his mother and sister.

"If I am not there soon, I will get arrested!"

"Stop crying, stinky," Connie interrupted. "Mum bought a bigger place so her convict son will have more space to run around in for a year."

"You did, mum? How did you know I would get home detention?"

"I still have some influence left, Jordan," she said, as she drove the quiet Jaguar saloon onto the freeway. "I knew two weeks ago you would get home detention, so I bought this place and cleared it with the court this morning."

"You knew I wasn't going to jail for two weeks and you didn't tell me?" he replied in a strangled voice. His anger was rising. "I have been scared witless for a fortnight, hoping I would not get sent there and you knew?"

"If you are looking for an apology young man, you won't be getting one," exclaimed Claire, her voice controlled, but angry. "You did the crime and now you are going to do the time and in a much larger house, so thanks for your appreciation!"

Jordan realised that his mother had done something very nice for him and all he had done was yell at her.

"Sorry, mum," he said. "I really do appreciate what you are doing. I've been stupid and I know you are only trying to help."

"That's okay, Jordan," she said, her voice now calm and maternal. "I wasn't supposed to know about it either. I pulled a few strings and I found out you were getting detention just two weeks ago, but I couldn't tell you because technically, it is improper to know."

"Oh, okay," he replied. "That makes sense, I guess."

"And she also wanted you to suffer, convict!" spat Connie.

Jordan said nothing and simply took the barb.

She probably did want me to suffer too. And she wouldn't have been wrong. This is the stupidest thing I've ever done.

Unfortunately, that was true. There was a solid history of misbehaviours and foolish actions by Jordan over the past few years, culminating in his ill-considered and ill-fated burglary. He had been suspended several times from school for cheating, for bullying some of the little kids and was nearly expelled once. He was a small teenager himself and was often teased about it from friends and classmates and rather than take it the good-natured way it had been given, he would take it out on the much younger students who were significantly smaller than himself.

Rather than use his very smart brain to study and do homework, he resorted to cheating and plagiarising which had led to him being taken out of high school before completing his final year. Not that he was ever going to pass his final exams. He simply hadn't worked very hard.

Jordan was lazy, undisciplined and childish.

And he still wet the bed every night.

"I think you will like the new house, Jordan. It has five bedrooms and is larger than the old one, but best of all, it is on four thousand square metres of land, so you will be allowed anywhere on it, as long as you don't cross a fence."

The making of a baby

Jordan was silent and taken aback. His biggest fear of home detention was of going stir crazy inside a small home with only a little area outside and now, he was going to live in what sounded like a paradise of space.

Over the last few months, he had tried to imagine what it would be like confined to a cell and with an exercise yard full of bigger and scarier people than him. It terrified him and his fears had turned into not only wetter beds, but smellier ones that had earned him his new nickname of 'stinky'.

A four thousand square metre property sounded like heaven compared to the prison hell he had imagined. It would still be tough being denied the ability to leave, but it already sounded far better than his old compact, inner-city home.

Jordan began to smile. In a day full of fears and terror, there was finally something to be pleased about.

Barnsdale was a very small town not far out of the city. It was one of those towns that had long since been encroached on by freeways and urban expansion, but it was still quaint and quiet compared to the noise and density of the inner city. Most of the homes were older and larger and most housing blocks were sizable, something that was increasingly rare in the city itself.

Jordan looked out the window of the Jaguar and watched the freeway disappear and the smaller side roads emerge until finally, they were on a narrow road where cars could pass only at low speed and with some difficulty. The Jaguar XJ was a large car and it was fortunate that they came across no other vehicles.

Watching the road slowly go by, Jordan sighed at the loss of his driving licence. It had been suspended somewhat pointlessly for the duration of his detention. He couldn't drive anywhere anyhow beyond up and down the driveway – assuming the new house even had one.

"Here we are," announced Claire, as they left the road and drove through the double wrought-iron gates and down the short driveway.

The making of a baby

The house was a timber and stone residence less than fifty years old with a slate path up to the front door. It looked rustic but well maintained and it had substantial gardens, something that Jordan immediately appreciated. He wasn't really a fan of gardens normally, but it hit him then that these gardens would be the entirety of his outside world for the next twelve months.

He suddenly appreciated them very much.

"We have our beds and a tiny bit of furniture for now," Claire explained, as she opened the front door. "The rest of our belongings will arrive tomorrow with the removalists."

Jordan walked in and began to explore the house with his mother by his side. It was roughly twice the size of their old home.

"This is my room," she said, pointing to the moderate-sized front bedroom. "And I have an en-suite bathroom and a walk-in 'robe."

Down the hall, right next to Claire's room was Connie's new bedroom. It was a larger room, with a large double window that made it very light and airy.

"Your room, for now, is just here," his mother announced, opening the solid timber door.

Jordan walked into a sparse, if largish, room that had nothing but his old bed and a small wardrobe in it. Their previous home had been very modern and well-lit while this new house was showing its age a bit and had poorly lit areas in most rooms. But Jordan was incredibly relieved to see his new room just the same. It was twice the size of the cell he had been expecting and it didn't have a grubby stainless-steel toilet on one wall either. It looked like paradise.

The next bedroom had been allocated to Claire as her personal study and was the smallest of the bedrooms.

"One more room to show you, Jordan," his mother said, and she opened the door to the largest bedroom in the house and clearly, what was once the master bedroom.

The making of a baby

It was decorated as a baby's nursery and also had a large en-suite bathroom with both a bath and a shower as well as a toilet.

Unlike the rest of the house, no expense had been spared in the decorating of this exquisite baby's nursery. The walls were decorated in pastels and pinks. Cartoon animals featured around the room. There were multiple shelves where teddy bears, toys and dolls once sat. Along one wall was a large built-in wardrobe that was empty. The floor was thickly carpeted, and the lighting was modern and dimmable.

It was by far, the best decorated and renovated room in the house. Clearly, the parents had loved and cared for their baby very much.

"What do you think, Jordan?" she asked curiously.

"It's very pretty," he replied, not really sure why she cared for his opinion about a room they would never use as it currently was.

"All it needs is a cot and a change table and of course, a baby and everything is ready."

"Yeah, I guess," he grunted.

Jordan was exhausted by the emotional upheavals of the day.

"Would you mind if I just went and had a nap, mum? I'm exhausted."

"Sure thing baby," she said, sweetly. Her maternal voice had returned now they were home. Her self-assured, confident and somewhat unfeeling voice and nature, were her public persona, her protection against the world. At home, however, she was a happy and maternal woman who cared for the well-being of both her children.

"Your bed is protected, so you can have a good sleep."

Protected.

Jordan winced at the word 'protected'. He knew what it meant, precisely. As he slipped off his clothes and pulled back the quilt of his single bed, stuck in the middle of a room with nothing else in it, he half expected the plastic sheet on his mattress to crackle as it did every time he got in. But there was no crackle.

She got me a new waterproof! How cool is that?

Lying in the bed, he could still tell there was a plastic under-sheet, the protection he had only briefly been without for a couple of months, before his father's death had brought the flooding back once again. Before his exhaustion claimed him, he lifted the corner of the sheet to see his new non-crackly plastic protector.

Shit! It's pink! And it has teddy bears on it!

He was surprised and humiliated by the sight of the babyish waterproof on his bed.

They are just teasing me about the 'panties' thing. I know it!

He laid back on the pillow and just seconds later, fell into a deep sleep, the day's traumatic events having taken their toll.

Jordan had a history with panties. A long and not very attractive one. When he was ten years old, he had stolen his sister's panties and foolishly worn them to bed and had, of course, wet them. He was easily caught. Over the years that followed, he continued to take her panties and wear them whenever he could. He also stole panties from a clothesline on the way to school and raided clothes dryers in a communal laundry. By the time he was sixteen, his panty fetish had been the biggest issue of the argument between him and his mother, even topping his heavy bedwetting and indiscreet masturbation.

A year earlier, Claire had given up the battle and bought him his own panties to wear on the promise he would steal no more, a promise he had kept - until he committed the burglary that had nearly landed him in jail.

Along with nightly wet sheets, Claire had the unpleasant task of washing his wet panties, often noticing that the wetness was not just urine.

When discussing her issues with Jordan with her own therapist, they had both decided that giving Jordan his own panties and possibly considering a bra at some stage, was the best way to keep him from stealing them and getting into serious trouble. It had worked well until he had fallen in with Travis who was that day, 'enjoying' his first day in prison. Claire was not unhappy about that.

After his arrest, Claire began her own desperate search for a way of bringing her intelligent, but wayward son, back into line. It was then that she found a book by Amanda Marsden simply called, *Saving my Son*. A lightbulb went off and Claire began preparations for saving *her* son.

"*Saving my son*"

J ordan awoke two hours later to a very familiar feeling.

He was wet. Very wet.

His deep sleep had left him in a wet patch that reached past his knees and extended just short of his pillow. It was relatively rare for him to wet his bed during a daytime nap, but not unheard of.

"You will just have to sleep in it tonight," exclaimed Claire, after he had gotten up and walked into the kitchen still wearing nothing but his wet boy's undies. "I won't have a washing machine

until tomorrow at the earliest and that is the only set of sheets I have here."

"Okay," he said, figuring they would easily dry out long before bedtime since it was still only early afternoon. "Do I have some dry... er..."

"Panties?" she suggested without a hint of condemnation. Claire had moved past feeling frustration at his pantie-wearing.

"Yes, please. These are wet."

"I can see that," she remarked with a tinge of sarcasm. "Connie!" she yelled. "Can you loan Jordan a pair of panties, please?"

The pee-wet boy went red at the open mention of his pantie-wearing. It was not exactly a secret, but hardly a matter of family discussion. Reminding his sister about it was even worse. And the irony was thick that his mother was asking his sister to loan him some panties, given that was how the whole 'panties' thing had begun so many years earlier.

"Here you go, panty-boy," said Connie, handing him a pair of yellow panties with a bow in front. Her face was smirking. "Don't make a mess in them!"

The comment was an obvious reference to days gone past where he would wear her panties and masturbate into them. He hadn't done that since he had his own girls' underwear, but she still remembered and made mention of it whenever she could.

"The rest of our clothes and furniture will be here in the morning, so Connie will give you another pair in the morning unless you are perhaps planning on *not* wetting your bed for a change?"

Jordan left the humiliating discussion on his bedwetting and his panties and went to his new room to get dressed. It was convenient for him that he and Connie shared the same size of underwear. His sister, however, thought otherwise.

As he explored the sizable backyard of his new home, Jordan felt a great sense of relief. Four thousand square metres was not a

The making of a baby

huge amount of area to be confined in for a year, but it beat a cell and an exercise yard by a very large margin. The ground sloped gently down to the back fence and there were a lot of trees, some semi-established gardens, and a large lawned area.

This won't be too bad at all. I can do it. I just have to get through it and then move on.

That evening, the three members of the family sat in the living room, reading books and magazines. Connie mainly used her tablet computer. Since his arrest, Jordan had been banned from computers and the internet totally. For the first couple of months of his ban, it felt like he was already in prison, but he had rediscovered his love of books and devoured them during the many internet-free hours he had. The television was still to be delivered along with their DVDs, so the room was unnaturally quiet, and the stillness of the semi-rural setting added to the sense of distance from everything. There was no sound of traffic or of people close and loud. Their neighbour's house was around a hundred metres away whereas before, the gap was less than two metres.

Before he went to bed, Jordan went to the toilet and sat down to masturbate as was his common ritual before bed. Normally, he would do this in his own room, with his own panties and his collection of printed porn and the pleasure of his vast array of fantasies. But that night, his room had none of those objects and so the toilet was his pleasure place. As he ejaculated, he felt more than sexual release. All of his fears and worries overwhelmed him and he silently cried. There was much to still fear, even now that prison had been avoided. He was still himself, and he scared himself with his laziness and inability to concentrate. It had been his weaknesses that had put him on the path of burglary and in his sessions with Doctor Woods, he admitted that he was easily led. That hadn't changed. He was safe for a year, but after that, he was still a boy with not as much control as he should have. And he still had all of the inner disturbances and imbalances he had always failed to control.

He was still scared.

When he went to his sparse bedroom, he stripped down to Connie's yellow panties and slid into the dry, but stained bed. He cried briefly before his tiredness claimed him and he slept solidly until the morning, not waking even once.

"How's my little boy this morning?" were the first words he heard the next morning. It was his mother standing beside his bed.

"What time is it?" he asked groggily.

"Time for my little bedwetter to get up!"

His mother never came into his room without knocking. This was new.

Claire pulled back the quilt to reveal Jordan's very wet bed. It was as it appeared every morning – soaking wet.

"Up you get, please," she ordered. "You need to go and have a shower quickly. The removalists will be here in an hour and you need to be dressed and ready to help."

Claire pulled a clean pair of panties out of her pocket and put them on his pillow next to his still half-asleep head.

"Here are some fresh panties for you. Now hurry up and shower. Leave the sheets on the bed to dry out. I won't get to washing today, so you will have to sleep in it again."

"Again?" he complained.

His mother gave him a withering look. "If you wet your bed, you can sleep in it. Don't blame me. Now go and get clean and dressed.

The shared bathroom was quite functional, but nowhere near as pristine and functional as the old one. The shower took a while to warm up and while the bathroom was large, it was cold.

As he showered, he was still deeply relieved that he was waking up to a cold bathroom instead of a cold cell and a cold wet bed.

The making of a baby

"Did you like my panties, stinky?" teased Connie, as they stood outside awaiting the removalists to commence unloading.

"They are fine," he replied before adding, "And thanks for letting me have them. I had nothing else to wear."

Their sibling relationship was testy at times, but Connie still cared for Jordan and like every other sister, wanted to help him. In this case, it meant loaning him her panties.

"Well, that's about to change!" Connie said. The first of the boxes of personal items, including their clothes – and Jordan's ten pairs of girl's panties – were being moved into the house. "Your *panties* are in that box!" she whispered.

Jordan's embarrassment continued as his bed was left open to dry off while men moved a number of boxes into his room. His status of 'bedwetter' was being exposed to others yet again. Not that it was exactly a huge secret in his family or with a number of his friends.

"Former friends," he thought glumly.

His arrest and their moving house effectively terminated all his previous friendships. A few of them knew he wet the bed courtesy of sleepovers and even an afternoon nap at one place.

A couple of hours later, everything had been delivered and the unpacking had commenced.

Jordan's clothes – and beloved panties – didn't quite fit into the old wardrobe in his bedroom, but most of them did. He had a dedicated drawer for them along with his socks. His porn magazines were in a box of his books and he blushed as he realised his mother had packed them during the two days he was away from home during his two court appearances and hotel stays. The hotel had put down a plastic sheet for him and he had dutifully soaked the bed on both nights.

He thought he had hidden his porn well, but when his room had been emptied, the small hidden area behind one drawer which held his stash had been discovered. While his mother and sister were

The making of a baby

unpacking the rest of the boxes, he quickly opened his magazines and a few minutes later unloaded onto his still wet sheets.

Dinner that night was pizza, delivered to their door not long after dark. While the kitchen was fully set up, no one wanted to cook after a day of unpacking.

"Jordan, can you come to your room, please?" his mother suddenly announced, early that evening.

Jordan looked up from the sci-fi book he had been enjoying.

"Why?"

"Just do as you are told, please. Go to your room and I will meet you there."

Unhappily, he closed his book and stalked off to his room. As he turned on the light, he froze in mid-step. In the middle of his now dry – but stained bed - was an already-folded, terry towelling nappy.

"In you go," said his mother, pushing him from behind.

"What this?" demanded Jordan.

"It's a nappy obviously," she answered. "And from now on, you will be wearing one."

"No, I won't," he replied, defiantly.

"Do I need to remind you that you are on home detention and that is effectively parole and if your parole officer finds you are being disobedient, it is off the jail for you?"

Jordan looked at her with wide-open eyes.

She wouldn't surely?

The look in her eyes made him unsure.

Maybe she would!

"Now get all your clothes off right now and lay on the nappy so I can pin it on properly."

Jordan was frozen in place.

"Now, young man!" she exclaimed.

"I can do it myself," he countered, in a quiet and meek voice.

"No, you can't," she replied. "You have wet the bed long enough and from now on, you will wear nappies. And I will put them on you unless you want your sister to do it!"

The thought of Connie seeing him in a nappy at all horrified him, but the idea of her pinning one on him was far, far worse. Slowly he stripped his clothes off until he was just in panties – his own panties.

"Panties off please," she demanded. "I've seen it all before, way too many times."

Jordan blushed, not just at stripping naked, but at the memory of being caught masturbating several times because of his carelessness. Now fully naked, he laid down on top of the kite-folded terry nappy.

"Slide down a bit more, please," she asked and he did as requested.

Claire pulled a container of baby powder from a bag she had brought in with her and began to sprinkle him liberally with it.

Jordan was terribly scared of getting an erection and so resorted to his two favourite boner-killing images – his grandmother and the Queen. Both had tremendous power in killing his arousal level. It worked.

"Now, baby, it is time for the pins!" she exclaimed and then expertly opened the top of the metal nappy pin, painted in bright pink and slid it through the material. Then she pinned the other side forming a perfectly fitting baby nappy on her teenage son.

"I think we better make sure you are safe tonight and she used two more pins to provide even more strength and no gaps around the legs."

"Well done, baby!" she announced. "The worst is over, but we have to put your plastic pants on now."

He had forgotten about plastic pants. A nappy without plastic pants was pretty much pointless. Claire took out a brand-new pair of plain pink plastic pants and flicked them open.

"Lift your legs please, so I can slide these on."

Jordan lifted his legs just enough for his mother to slide the pink plastic baby pants up his legs.

"Bottom up now," she demanded. And he did so, using his feet to lift his backside off the sheet below.

The pants slipped around the bulk of his nappy and Claire carefully made sure that his entire nappy was covered by the plastic protective pants.

"There," she said happily. "All done and now you are ready for bed."

"Bed, now?"

"Absolutely!"

"But it's only nine o'clock and I stay up until eleven!" he protested.

"From now on, you will go to bed when I say so, do you understand?"

"Yes mum," he replied grumpily. He figured it would not last long. Before long, he would be staying up late once more. He just had to weather the storm.

"Oh, I forgot one thing. You are also going to start wearing pyjamas. None of this walking around just in panties in the morning."

Out of the mysterious bag, Claire withdrew a pair of pink flannel pyjamas with prints of little animals on them.

"Now, put these on so you stay warm at night."

He just looked at them and didn't move. They were girls' pyjamas. Not that he actually objected to them as they were kind of cute, but his interest in such things was still hidden, he thought. But more importantly, they were pyjamas for little girls, while being in an impossibly large size.

Jordan was overwhelmed by everything and once again began to cry.

"I'm sorry mum," he sobbed. "I'm sorry for everything I've done."

"I know you are, Jordan," she added, her face softening as she saw his tears. "But I have to help you become a better person and for now, you are wearing these pyjamas. Let me help you with them."

While Jordan softly cried, Claire helped him into his pyjama tops and did up the buttons. She then helped him put on his bottoms one leg at a time.

"You look very pretty, Jordan," she said softly. "Now get into bed and go to sleep."

Thoroughly beaten, he slipped under the quilt, while his mother tucked him in. The dried out wet sheet still had a slight aroma of pee.

"Now baby, that nappy does *not* come off, do you understand?" she reminded him. "I will take your nappy off myself in the morning and the same applies to the pyjamas. Both of them stay on until I change you. If you don't obey me, I will spank you."

In the middle of his emotional storm, Jordan fully believed that his mother would spank him as she had said, something she had not done since before his father had died.

Claire stood outside his bedroom for about five minutes, waiting for the sobbing and the deep sighing to cease. When they finally stopped and were replaced by the sound of deep breathing, she returned to the living room and picked up her copy of *Saving my Son* and started to read it for the third time.

There was still much to learn and to implement, but lesson one had been a success. Her wayward son was in a nappy.

"There is simply no way to fully explain the power of the nappy on a teenage boy. You have to experience it to fully appreciate what such a mundane object can achieve in terms of modifying bad behaviour. If your boy is still a bedwetter, then putting him in a nappy now makes sense. If he was a late bedwetter, you can still put him in one, because his wetting may return. If not, a nappy is still a powerful tool for saving your boy from trouble and violence ahead. You need to get him into a nappy as a first priority.

Yes, a nappy is a baby item and that, dear reader, is exactly the point."

Saving My Son: Chapter two

Discipline

" How are we this morning?" asked the impossibly cheery Claire, as she once again, stood by Jordan's bed early the next morning.

Not again... Why can't she let me sleep?

"Time to get you up for breakfast!"

Jordan glanced over at the digital clock he had rescued from the pile of his belongings. A lot of them still sat in boxes on the floor. It was 7:00 am.

"Is your bed dry?" she asked.

Jordan put his hands underneath him and for the first time in five years, his sheets were dry.

"Yep," he replied, nodding.

"Let me check your nappy," she said and pulled back the quilt and slipped her hand underneath his plastic pants. "Well you have a very wet nappy, young man, but not too bad for now. Breakfast is nearly ready, so get up and come now."

"I'll just get changed – "

"No, you won't!" interrupted his mother. "You can come for breakfast like this and I will change you later on."

Jordan went to say something and then thought better of it and walked sullenly behind his mother into the kitchen.

"I like your PJs," Connie said. Her face and manner declared that she was being honest. "Does he really have a nappy on, mum?" she asked.

"Jordan, you can answer that question."

Jordan mumbled a yes.

"Answer it properly, please. You have a voice."

"Yes, I'm wearing a nappy," he admitted, his face colour matching his pyjamas.

"Good for you!" his sister replied. "Good for you. Must be a lot comfier than wet sheets."

"I guess so," he stammered. He really wasn't up for a discussion of the merits of wearing nappies with his sister.

As he sat down to some hot porridge and toast, Jordan began to relax. His mother and sisters both knew he liked and wore panties. That uncomfortable family conference was many years gone now. The pink PJs were actually quite nice, if a bit young in style.

The nappy isn't too bad, I guess. If it shuts everyone up, then so be it!

Breakfast was over too quickly.

"Let's go to your room now, Jordan," Claire announced. "Quickly please, I don't have all day."

Jordan walked to his room, unsure of what was about to happen. He was still in a quite wet nappy and had been told under threat of spanking, that he could not remove it.

"Now let's get you changed and dressed."

Claire began to undo his pyjama top buttons and slapped away his hands when he tried to do it himself.

"I'm getting you dressed, so keep your hands to yourself! Now, arms up so I can take it off."

He lifted his arms and his mother removed the PJ top and then pulled his bottoms down.

"Lift your foot, baby," she asked. "Now your other one! Good boy! Very proud of you!"

The childish banter was annoying him, but he was still too shell-shocked to fight it. His mother went to a cupboard in the hall and extracted a large plastic-coated mat and laid it on his bed. It was a changing pad.

"Lie down please," she asked, and Jordan laid down on the changing pad awaiting the next indignity.

She quickly pulled the plastic pants off and was assaulted by the smell of a very wet nappy.

"Phew baby!" she exclaimed. "That is one very smelly nappy you have on!"

But instead of a grimace or a scowl, she smiled at him sweetly and added. "Much better than a wet bed though, isn't it?"

She extracted the two pairs of pink nappy pins and the sodden nappy fell away. The effect of the warm nappy giving way to the cool air had the outcome he feared. He erected and his grandmother and the Queen were too late to stop it from happening.

Claire took no notice whatsoever.

She placed a new packet of baby wipes on his bedside cupboard and began to wipe him thoroughly. She didn't avoid any area and as she wiped his penis, Jordan prayed he would not embarrass himself.

He didn't. In fact, the opposite happened. As the wiping continued, his arousal reduced, until, by the time his mother declared the job done, he was flaccid and safe again.

"Well, that's done. Now let's get you a brand new, clean nappy and put that on."

"What!" he yelled indignantly. "I'm not wearing a nappy now. It's not bedtime, so I don't need one!"

Claire looked at him and her eyes narrowed.

"From now on, you will be wearing a nappy and I won't hear anything from you about it, do you understand?"

"I won't!" he yelled. "I won't do it."

"Yes, you will and if you fight me on it, I will get the wooden spoon and whack your bottom until you can't sit down!"

"You wouldn't dare!" he said defiantly, standing completely naked next to his bed.

"Connie!" she yelled, not taking her eyes off of him. "Would you bring the wooden spoon in here, please?"

Jordan looked at her in surprise. He wanted to run and to get away from everything, but he knew he couldn't. He was trapped.

"Here, mum!" said Connie, as his sister handed her the large kitchen wooden spoon.

"Thanks. Now close the door on your way out."

"Can't I –"

"No. This is between me and your baby brother."

As soon as the door closed, somewhat reluctantly, Claire looked at her son.

"Bend over the bed. Now!"

Jordan stood still, still unsure of what to do.

Claire swiftly hit his naked bottom with the wooden spoon once.

Jordan quickly put his hands on the bed and bent over.

Just outside the closed door, Connie listened intently.

"From now on, the rules are different," Claire said. "You will do whatever I say and if you defy me, I will spank you like a child. And this is the first time you are getting the wooden spoon for disobeying me."

WHACK!

Connie winced as she heard the solid report of the big kitchen spoon connecting with Jordan's backside.

WHACK!

She heard a slight whimper from her brother.

Claire rained down twenty-three more whacks with the wooden spoon on his bottom before finally stopping.

"Now you will stand there and not say a word while I fold your nappy."

Jordan stood still, his chest heaving as the tears flowed down his face, while Claire kite-folded a clean nappy on his bed.

"Hop on and let's finish this."

Jordan laid on the nappy, wincing with every repositioning of his very red backside while his mother once again pinned the nappy together. Another brand-new pair of pink plastic pants, these ones with tiny stars on them, were then pulled up and covered the nappy once again.

"Now, here are some panties to go over the top. Do you need help putting them on as well?" she asked.

"No, Mum," he replied, still sniffling.

"Then put them on and then a shirt and if you have any jeans that fit over your nappy, put them on as well. When you are dressed, we are going to sit outside and read for a while and you are going to join me."

He thought about complaining. He didn't want to go outside and just sit, reading a book with his mother. His sister was about to leave for work, and he wanted to do things on his own. But his still-tingling backside reminded him that he should do as he was told, at least for that day.

Jordan struggled to put his jeans on, the bulk of the nappy making the job considerably more difficult. Worse still, the nappy was very obvious under them. A person looking might not know exactly what he was wearing, but they would know he was wearing *something.*

It was a warm and beautiful day as mother and son sat on two reclining garden chairs outside in the sun, reading and resting. They had been there for a couple of hours when Jordan asked to be excused.

"Mum," he asked. "Can I go back inside now?"

Jordan didn't quite understand why he even had to ask permission, but it felt like the right thing. His bottom was still sending a strident message to his brain: *behave.*

"Why do you need to go inside?" Claire asked.

"I need to go to the toilet," he answered.

"For a pee or a poo?"

"A pee."

"Then use your nappy," his mother insisted. "That is why you have it on."

"But I can't wee in my nappy, mum!" he replied, with a whine.

"Of course, you can," she answered. "I put you in a nappy for a reason and so you will use it like a baby. Now, I don't want to hear any more silliness from you. It will be lunchtime soon and if you are wet, I will change you then."

Jordan's head spun at what she said.

She expects me to piss my nappy instead of using a toilet? What happens when I need a poo?

Looking away from his mother and pretending to stare at a tree by the fence, Jordan relaxed his bladder and wet his nappy. His sense of relief was palpable.

That wasn't as bad as I thought it would be. I hope my panties are still dry!

Mummy

 Time for lunch I think," announced Claire suddenly, sitting up and closing her book.

"Would you like some sandwiches to eat, baby?"

"Yes please, mum."

"Stay here and don't wander off the lawn. I need to know where you are at all times."

Jordan was confused. His mother was treating him like he was three years old again, making him stay in one place as if he couldn't be trusted on his own. It was annoying him. She wasn't even allowing him to wander the garden without her.

Ten minutes later, she returned with a plate of freshly made sandwiches and two glasses of lemonade. He ate his portion voraciously.

"Mum," he said carefully. "I am going to go look around the garden."

He wasn't exactly asking for permission, but he was putting it out there just the same.

"Just wait a few minutes until I have finished lunch and then I will go with you."

Jordan sighed. He felt like his mother was 'taking him for a walk'.

Claire stood up and grabbed her son's hand as they walked down the path that led to the back fence.

"It's a pretty garden, isn't it?" she said.

"Yes, it is. It's a lot better than our old place."

"It looks like I will need to do some gardening back here," she mentioned. "And you can help me. I will ask Connie to get me some more plants and we can fill out some of the empty places. Would you like that?"

"Yeah, I think so," he replied, as his mother squeezed her grip on his hand.

"If you are a good boy, you can help me plant some vegetables down in the other corner and we can have our own fresh veggies. Would you like to do that with me, baby?"

"Yes, mum," he replied again. He didn't know what else to do or say.

Claire held her son's hand tightly as they wandered the gardens, checking on all the plants and trees, seeing where some weeding was required and discussing new plants. She only briefly let go of his hand when she pulled a few weeds or looked behind a particularly scruffy plant to see what lay behind it.

The making of a baby

As they were walking, Jordan wet his nappy once again and grinned slightly. It was a silly grin. He felt the warmth spread around his nappy and it felt oddly comfortable, despite the tightness of his jeans.

A few minutes later as they were walking back to the house, Claire stopped and put her hand down the back of his jeans and underneath his plastic pants.

"Baby, you are wet. Let's get you back to your room for a quick change."

Holding his hand once again, she led him up the path and over the lawn and back inside the house and was soon in his bedroom. Without waiting to be asked, she sat him on the bed and took off his shoes and slid down his jeans.

"I think we need to get you some more clothes that fit over a nappy better," she commented. "Now lie back down again on the changing pad and let's get this wet nappy off, shall we?"

He laid down as ordered and his mother quickly pulled his panties and plastic pants off and then proceeded to unpin his nappy.

"Isn't it better to use your nappy than that nasty old toilet, baby?" she asked.

"I don't know," he answered, numbly. "It was okay, I guess."

Claire continued to talk to him while she skilfully wiped him clean, slipped a folded nappy under his bottom and pinned it together. As she pulled up yet another brand-new pair of pink patterned plastic pants, Jordan asked her a question.

"Mum, why are you making me wear a nappy like a baby?"

"Because you wet the bed. You know that already."

As she answered, she slipped his t-shirt off and put his pink pyjama top on.

"But I don't wet my pants during the day!" he objected weakly.

"Then what did I just take off you then, huh?" she said. "That was one very wet nappy for a boy that doesn't wet his pants!"

She held up his pyjama bottoms and told him to step in.

"But why do you call me 'baby'? And why do I have to wear pyjamas now?"

Jordan was upset with everything that was going on. Nothing made sense anymore. Claire leaned over to hug him.

"I call you 'baby' because you still are a bit of a baby and I think you know it. You wet the bed. You act silly at times and you even broke into someone's house like you were a silly child. So, for a while, I am going to help you feel a bit better and to start with, you are going to wear nappies and plastic pants."

"But I don't want to, mummy!" he cried. "I don't want to go to sleep now! I don't want to!"

"There, there, little baby," she said, patting his back, as he cried once again. "Looks like my little baby needs a sleep. Jump into bed and let me tuck you in."

Feeling stupid, but also very oddly happy, Jordan slipped into bed and Claire tucked him in and kissed him on the forehead.

"Have a good sleep, little baby," she whispered to him. "Mummy is just in the other room."

She walked out smiling.

"He called me 'mummy'," she thought to herself. "He is starting to act more like a baby than he was."

Claire was thrilled he had called her 'mummy'. It made her feel like she was regaining some control over her wayward son and partway towards sorting him out properly.

Jordan slept almost two hours and when he awoke, he felt safe and secure and noticed that once again, his nappy was wet. When he put his hand inside his plastic pants, he felt the surprising dampness. He had no recollection of wetting his nappy during his nap.

The making of a baby

"Look who's up!" exclaimed Claire, as a still sleepy Jordan wandered into the living room. "Did you forget that you aren't allowed to get up on your own? Come over here baby, let me check you."

He walked over to his mother who immediately put her hand inside his plastic pants.

"Hmmm, just damp for now. You don't need a change just yet. You can play for a little while."

Play? What does she mean by play?

"I put some of your old Lego sets in the nursery. Why don't you go and see how they are for a while? Your sister will be home in a couple of hours."

Jordan wandered down to the nursery and once again as he walked in, he was taken aback by the stunning room. While there was no nursery furniture in it such as a cot, change table, playpen and of course, baby toys, it was still a lovely bright and airy room.

Sitting in one corner were three plastic tubs with his old Lego blocks and sets.

Feeling suddenly at peace, he grabbed one of the tubs and brought it to the middle of the room and emptied it on the floor. Sitting cross-legged in his damp nappy and pink girl's pyjamas, he started to build with his Lego, just as he had only a few years before.

Two hours passed quickly as he engrossed himself in building and creating and making cars, trucks, planes and small towns. A few times, Claire silently crept to the nursery door and watched her son playing – playing with toys and smiling. A single tear ran down her face.

"I will save my son," she repeated silently from the book she had been reading. "I will save my son."

Thirty minutes later, Claire wandered into the nursery holding a fresh nappy and the changing pad.

The making of a baby

"Time for a nappy change, baby!" she announced cheerfully.

Jordan looked at her and smiled. He knew the ritual now and was no longer terrified of it. Lying on the thickly carpeted floor of the amazing nursery, he happily let his mother unpin his surprisingly wet nappy, wipe him up intimately, powder him all over and pin a new one. The Queen and his Grandmother were not needed this time as his penis did not even stir. He was thinking largely about his Lego project, not the fact that his mother was changing his nappy.

"You look like you are having fun... for a convict," shouted Connie, walking into the nursery not long after.

Jordan looked up at her and she was smiling. There was no malice in her voice.

"I haven't played with my Legos for years," he said, genuinely happy. "It could be worse, that's for sure."

"How come you are in your PJs already?" she asked. "Is mum putting you to bed this early?"

"No, I don't think so," he replied. "I had a nap and I wore them to bed and I haven't changed out of them yet."

"So, it's not just panties you like?" his sister asked.

"I guess not," he replied. "If I have to wear pyjamas at all, I like these."

"So, I need to hide my bras too?" she said, with a laugh.

Jordan blushed slightly.

"Really?" she exclaimed in surprise. "Well at least ask first before you steal them!"

Jordan shrugged and Connie came to sit down on the floor with him.

"Mum's really pissed with you," she said. "She cried every day after you got arrested."

"I... I didn't know that," he said.

"And she wasn't the only one, you prick!" she spat out.

"Sorry," he muttered.

"I heard mum belt your arse this morning," she said with a cheeky grin. "She's been wanting to do that for years now and you gave her the perfect opportunity coz you can't run away!"

"Yeah, I know, it still stings!"

"You better behave because she has a proper paddle now!"

Jordan's eyes widened.

"She has a spanking paddle?"

"Yep, she showed it to me a few days ago. If you get that thing, you won't sit down for a week!"

"Shit!" he exclaimed. "I better try and avoid it!"

"I don't like your chances, stinky convict. You are a marked man." Then she looked at his obvious nappy bulge. "Or should I say, marked baby!"

"I don't know why mummy is making me wear a nappy," he said.

"Did you just call her 'mummy'?" she said. "Now you are talking like a baby!"

"I meant 'mum'. She's making me wear a nappy. She won't let me use the toilet!"

"Well you do wet the bed and you pee during your naps so... why not?"

"I don't wet my pants though. So, I don't need a nappy."

"I wouldn't push it, Jordan," Connie said standing up to leave. "I'd worry a bit more about when you need to do a poo."

Jordan hadn't considered that part. Now he was starting to worry even more.

Bath toys

As Jordan sat at the table for dinner, he was very conscious that he was in a nappy and still in his pink pyjamas. He felt slightly silly, but at least Connie was being nice to him and he felt as if he had an ally of sorts against his mother's babying of him. The thought of the proper spanking paddle terrified him somewhat. But after his fears of prison and what his backside might be subject to in there, even the paddle wasn't quite as frightening as it might otherwise have been.

He was quiet and subdued while his mother and Connie talked about all manner of topics. He was still trying to find his feet during his home detention and how he could fit back into the household. Being made to wear nappies was incredibly awkward and embarrassing, but at least he felt safe again, something he hadn't felt since his arrest.

As the last mouthful of ice cream was swallowed, Claire announced that it was time for Jordan's bath.

"You want me to have a bath? What's wrong with the shower?"

She threw him another of her withering looks. Connie kicked him under the table to remind him that his mother possessed a new and potent spanking weapon.

"Come into the bathroom and I will get your bath ready for you," she continued. "You haven't had a bath all day and you've had three wet nappies. And I assume you are wet again?"

He blushed to confirm that he was indeed, wet again. He might not have felt wet, but during his ice cream, he had wet his nappy once more. It surprised him just how easy it had been and how he was wetting before he even knew it.

"Connie, will you please clear the table, while I bathe your baby brother?"

She's going to bathe me too? What next?

Jordan stood in the bathroom watching his mother put the plug in the bottom of the large cast-iron bath and turn on the water.

"But why can't I have a shower?" he repeated.

"Because I can't trust you yet and so for a while, you are going to have baths. Now if you keep complaining, I will have to wash you as well," she said firmly, daring him to argue. "So, are you going to have a bath?"

"Yes, mum," he said, unhappily.

The making of a baby

He stood there as his mother took off his pyjamas, pulled down his panties and plastic pants and then unpinned his wet nappy, allowing it to fall on the floor. He stood there shivering and naked waiting for the bath to fill.

"Now remember to wash yourself properly while you are in there and don't just play!" she told him. "I have a few toys you might like to play with."

Claire opened a brand-new packet of plastic bath toys for toddlers and put them in the bath. There were turtles, blocks, cars and other shapes.

"I will be back to check on you later, so make sure you wash and don't make too much of a mess."

Jordan sat in the hot water looking blankly at the baby toys floating in the bathtub with him.

"What am I supposed to do with these?" he said out loud, but quiet enough that no one else could hear. "I'm not a child! I don't need toys."

However, as he laid back in the water, the toys looked familiar and he began to pull them underwater and watch them fly back up to the surface. The blocks had holes in them so he could fill them full of water and then squeeze it out, imagining that the block was a rocket. By the time his mother came to get him out of the bath, he was happily playing with the toys and unhappy that it was time to get out.

"It looks like you've been having fun, baby," commented his mother, after walking in silently and watching him playing for a few minutes.

Jordan looked back at her with an odd grin. "Yeah, I have. Do I have to get out yet, mummy?"

"There's that word 'mummy' again," thought Claire to herself. "Amanda was right about that."

"You can stay in the bath for ten more minutes, baby," said Claire. "But then you are getting out and getting your nappy and pyjamas on."

"Thank you," he said and turned to play with the bath toys some more.

Claire knelt down next to the bath and grabbed a toy boat. She pushed it around the water while Jordan pushed a toy car at the same time. For a few precious moments, mother and son played with the bath toys together and smiled at each other.

Ten minutes later, he stepped out of the bath and his mother greeted him with a large fluffy towel and gave him a cursory wipe over.

"Now, finish drying yourself, baby, and then go to your bedroom so I can get you ready for bedtime."

"Do I have to go to bed yet, mummy?" he said, using the childish word once more.

"No, baby. Not yet," she said. "If you behave well, you can stay up for another hour."

When he got to his room, Claire once again folded a thick terry nappy and had him lie down on it.

"Do you like the powder, baby?" she asked.

"It's nice, mummy," he replied. "It smells nice and feels kind of funny!"

Jordan grinned as his mother dumped even more baby powder on him, before pinning the thick nappy together.

"Now let me look at what plastic pants to put on my baby! Hmmm... Which ones would you like to wear, baby?"

Claire held up two still brand-new pairs of plastic pants – one white with teddy bears drawn on them or an almost clear one.

"Can I have the teddy bears please, mummy?" he asked, a smile forming across his face.

"Of course," Claire replied, flicking the pants out and then expertly sliding them up Jordan's legs and over his nappy. "They are adorable, aren't they?"

Jordan nodded.

Claire was shocked by what had just happened. In the book, *Saving My Son*, the author had written that if you try to baby your son, there will be moments when he will just embrace it suddenly and without warning. This was what was happening now. Jordan was calling her *mummy* repeatedly, playing with baby toys and even enjoying a nappy change. The book encouraged her to make the best of these moments when they came and to push the boundaries. She also warned that later on, they will push back on what has happened, but not back to the beginning. It was a case of *'push and then retreat slightly, then push again'*.

"Your other pyjamas are in the wash now, baby so I have some nice new ones I think you will like."

Claire held out the PJ top for Jordan to see. It was a white flannelette with printed teddy bears on it and some embroidered animals around the neck. Just above the heart, was 'Mummy's Baby', also embroidered in pink cotton.

Claire held her breath to see if her son would accept or reject the obviously babyish garment and was pleased to see him smile. As before, she dressed him in the pyjamas herself and buttoned up the top. She then put on some thick white socks to keep his feet warm.

"You look lovely and cosy, Jordan," she said, standing him up. "What do you think, Connie?"

Connie had ventured into the doorway of the bedroom, arriving just after the nappy was pinned on. She had watched her brother meekly submit to being dressed in very childish pyjamas.

The making of a baby

"They look really cute, Jordan," she said, still stunned that he had allowed his mother to literally dress him in that manner.

"Now you have an hour before you have to go to bed. Do you want to go and play in the nursery or read a book?"

"Play," he said.

Connie and Claire watched dumbfounded as Jordan padded his way to the nursery and happily sat on the floor to play with his Lego sets for the allocated hour.

"How have you gotten him to wear a nappy and be so... you know... happy?" asked Connie, once they were back in the living room.

"Jordan didn't grow up properly," she said. "I see it now that he just didn't get everything he needed and so I am giving it to him now."

"While he can't run away, you mean?" laughed Connie

"Well, yes, that is part of it, but Jordan needs some time to grow up again and get things sorted out."

"I don't really understand, but in the last couple of days he has been less of a pain in the arse than usual!"

"The hard stuff is still to come, but it was good he took to nappies so easily. That saves on some of the washing."

"I don't really mind him borrowing my undies sometimes, mum. But I think he will be wanting a bra soon. He kind of admitted it to me today."

Claire sighed. "I figured that might come, but someone wearing nappies doesn't need a bra, at least not yet. But there is something he does need, and I hope he will take it. He seems to be in a good place now, so it is time to try."

"Try what?"

From her pocket, Claire extracted a pink adult-size baby's dummy and held it up.

The making of a baby

"You want him to use a dummy?" Connie said, spitting out the words. "Really?"

"I do. I think it will comfort him and the time is right."

"They make adult dummies?" she asked, her voice tinged with incredulity.

"They are sold by the million so, yes, they do."

The two women read in silence while Jordan played with Lego, sitting on the floor of the unoccupied nursery. Claire opened *Saving my Son* to a specific passage that spoke to her day.

'A big mistake is to think that when you are trying to baby your son that it will all be in one direction and smooth going. Some days, you will wonder what you did right as he progresses quickly through the program and then be surprised that the next day, he has taken a step back. And some days, there will be nothing but pushback on the program.

You need to be resilient and understand that progress is not linear and always upwards. It is not always up. It is up and down, forward and backwards and times of no change at all. But over time, you will look back and see how far you have come. If every week, every month, you can see that your boy is more of a baby than he was before, then you are making fine progress. Enjoy the days where he wants more of it and embraces childhood and infancy and suffer through the days of rejection and difficulty. It is a big thing you are doing and a powerful and exceptional task you have committed to. I never said it would be easy. It may be quick; it may be slow, but it will never be easy."

"Time for bed, baby!" announced Claire. Jordan was still busy playing with his Lego. She noticed though that instead of complex buildings or vehicles, he had mainly built towers and simple structures.

"Okay, mummy," he said. Claire bent down and took his hand and helped him to his feet.

"I love your new jammies!"

"Me too!"

Claire took him by the hand and walked him down the hall to his room.

"Under the quilt, you go!" she said, and Jordan slipped into the bed and laid down.

He was smiling.

"Let me tuck you in," she said, as she made sure the sheets and quilt were tight around his body. "Did you have a good day today?" she asked.

Jordan nodded.

Claire was very surprised by his answer since that day had been his first in nappies and he had taken a heavy hit with the wooden spoon early on.

"Tomorrow will be an even better day," she promised. "And I have something here that will help you to sleep even better."

Claire extracted the dummy from her pocket and held it close to his face. Jordan looked confused. He could tell it was a dummy but was unsure why he would need one.

Claire put the dummy at his mouth, but it remained closed. She pushed a little and his mouth slowly opened. Then she pushed it home.

"It will help you sleep a lot better, baby, so keep it in."

Jordan held the dummy in his mouth without moving, still unsure what to do with it. He was tiring quickly and then he sucked it. And then he sucked it again and a few moments later was sucking the dummy contentedly.

The making of a baby

"Just close your eyes, sweetheart," Claire said, in her most soothing and motherly voice. "Mummy will stay with you for a while."

Claire sat on the end of the bed holding Jordan's hand watching him suck on the dummy with his eyes closed. Minutes later, the sucking slowed and his breathing became shallower. Baby Jordan was asleep.

"That was incredible!" whispered Connie, as Claire silently closed the door to Jordan's bedroom. She had watched the final scenes from the gloom of the hallway.

"It was, wasn't it!" exclaimed her mother. "I didn't think he'd take a dummy, but it was worth a try."

"He hardly complained at all and he went to sleep so easily!" Connie added. "I only wish I could get to sleep so quickly. It takes me hours sometimes!"

"I have an extra dummy if you want to try one!"

Connie laughed. "Nah, I don't think so. It wouldn't work anyhow. I don't need nappies either, not like piss pants!"

The two women chatted amicably for a few minutes.

"Is Jordan a girl?" asked Connie. It was a serious question.

"I'm honestly not sure," Claire responded. "I don't think so, but he does like girl's things and his nappies and baby PJs are all girls things so who knows…"

"And he wants one of my bras someday, so maybe he is at least partly a girl. Do you think that is why he gets in so much trouble?"

Claire's eyes became damp. Tears threatened.

"I've always worried that I missed something in his growing up that caused him to run off the rails. And maybe being a girl is part of the things I missed, even if he is only partly girl."

"And the bedwetting thing?"

"I think he wets the bed because part of him never really grew up."

"And that's why you are putting him in nappies?" Connie asked.

"Yeah in part. But you saw him tonight. How old do you think he was acting?"

"About six years old or so, I'd say. No way I'd ever wear PJs like that now."

"I don't know what will happen, but his home detention is giving me a chance to try and get him sorted out again. I'm not going to waste it. But it is bedtime for me. Jordan isn't the only one who had a tiring day."

On her way to bed, she peered through Jordan's bedroom door and saw that the dummy was still in his mouth and he was rhythmically sucking it. She smiled.

It was only the early days of his Home Detention and she already had him in a nappy and sucking a dummy.

"Not a bad day's efforts!" she thought.

Parole Officer

Jordan woke up early the next morning and as he moved his head sideways, he felt the dummy that had fallen out of his mouth during the night.

What's this garbage? I'm not having a dummy!

He picked up the dummy and threw it towards the door.

The making of a baby

He slipped his own hand inside his nappy and found he was once again, very wet. But he was also very aware of his bowels. It had been two days since the last time, and he was now very ready to empty out. But he remembered his mother's command to not get out of bed before she said so. It was a conflict where he either got up early and took a dump or he obeyed her and pooed his nappy.

He chose to risk getting up.

It was 6 am and his mother was still in bed, hopefully asleep. As he entered the toilet, he realised that he had never actually taken his own nappy off before and it was pinned so tight that it wouldn't just slide it down. He carefully extracted two pins from one side and was able to slip the nappy down to his ankles so he could complete his task. Trying to repin the nappy, however, proved to be a very difficult task. Sliding pins through a wet nappy was much harder than a dry one and so, his effort was loose and he could only hope his mother would not notice.

7 am came around and Claire opened the bedroom door. The first thing she noticed was the dummy lying on the floor. She knew it hadn't fallen the five feet from the bed to the door. It had been thrown.

"What's this doing here?" she asked.

"I didn't want it, so I threw it away," Jordan replied testily.

"You didn't mind it last night," she replied calmly.

"Mum, I'm not having a dummy!" he exclaimed loudly.

"Well the pushback has come already," Claire thought to herself. "I just wished it hadn't."

"Let's get your nappy changed first and get you dressed for the day," she said, trying to sound calm and collected.

"I can do it myself!" he shouted.

"Do I need to get the wooden spoon again, young man?" she threatened.

He shook his head meekly. Claire pulled off his PJ bottoms, laid him on the changing pad and slid down his plastic pants.

"What's this?" she exclaimed. "Did you take your nappy off yourself?"

"I had to, mum!" he pleaded. "I needed to have a poo and you weren't awake yet!"

"Then you should have done your poo in your nappy!" she responded, angrily. "What do you think a nappy is for anyhow? Pee and poo. Both!"

"I'm not going to poo in a nappy, mum!" he shouted angrily. "Never!"

"I have put you back in nappies for a purpose and you *will* use them properly!"

"I don't want to!" he said, less defiantly and with more pleading.

"It doesn't matter what *you* want, young man," she replied. "You do what I say when I say it!"

"But I don't want to poo in a nappy, mum," he said. "I don't mind weeing, but I don't want to poo, please."

Claire was unmoved.

"Stay here and don't move. I will teach you not to disobey me and to yell at me. Now bend over the bed and stay there."

Jordan quivered at the thought of the wooden spoon yet again, but he bent over and put his hands on the bed.

Connie had heard the commotion and watched her mother stride back into the bedroom holding her new unused paddle. This time the door was left open and she watched as the first strike hit home.

"Mummy, please!" he yelled.

WHACK

———————————◗◯◖———————————

"Mummy, I will behave, I promise!"

WHACK

"Sorry, mummy, please stop!"

WHACK

Silently Claire was pleased that 'mummy' had made a return.

WHACK

Thirty hits with the paddle on his wet behind, left his bottom cheeks glowing red. Jordan was sobbing with free-flowing tears. It was far harder than the previous day's spanking.

"Now lie down and let me get your nappy on," she demanded.

Jordan instantly complied, wincing every time his bottom came in contact with the nappy. Nothing more was said as Claire pinned a clean nappy on him and pulled on his plastic pants.

"Get some panties and the rest of your clothes on and come down for breakfast. Today, you have to meet your parole officer, so you need to be well-behaved."

Jordan said very little as he sat uneasily in his chair, still feeling the heat and sting of his spanking.

"I told you she had that paddle," whispered Connie to her brother as Claire briefly disappeared into the kitchen. "Why'd you misbehave?"

"I had to have a shit and I wasn't going to do it in the nappy!" he replied unhappily.

"How'd that work out, genius?" she said smugly, just as their mother returned.

"You have a 10 am appointment with your parole officer, so make sure your teeth and hair are brushed. You shouldn't need a nappy change before then."

The making of a baby

"Well, Mr Airesdale," said the parole officer, as she sat down at her desk. She was holding his file. "I see this is our first time together and we will be seeing each other each month and I am warning you now, I will drop in unannounced sometimes and if you are not home… off to jail, you go. Do you understand?"

"Yes, Miss," he replied.

"Mrs, if you don't mind. But I'd prefer it if you just called me Sophie. This is hard enough already and we don't need to be enemies. I am here to make sure you complete your sentence and then help you move on to better things."

Sophie stared at Jordan intently, before continuing.

"If you need medical appointments, you need to ring me for permission first and I will record it so there are no issues. Emergencies – genuine emergencies – are an exception and you are also allowed to go to church for an hour and a half once a week, but you need to let me know where and when."

"Am I allowed to use the internet?" he asked.

"There is nothing in the court's judgment that says you can't. Why do you ask?"

"Mum won't let me use it and she stopped me after I was arrested."

"Well there is a higher authority than the court and that is your mum, so unless you can change her mind, I can't do anything about that!"

Sophie smiled. Jordan was a sweet boy and she was trying to help him as best she could. Unlike some parole officers, she still believed that most people were good and getting in trouble was not the end of their lives.

The making of a baby

She suddenly stopped talking and stared at him again.

"Look, I have to ask this, Jordan," she said. "Are you wearing a nappy?"

Jordan's eyes went wide in shock.

"Why do you ask?" he stammered.

"I have a seven-year-old boy who still wears nappies at times, so I kind of recognised the shape of your trousers."

Jordan blushed slightly. "Yes, I am."

"May I ask why?"

"I wet the bed still."

"I already know that. It is in your file."

"It is?" Jordan was shocked and embarrassed.

"Yes, it is written here, but why are you wearing nappies during the day?"

Jordan looked down at his feet and mumbled. "Mum makes me wear them."

"Because she is mad at you for what you did?"

"Yeah, she says I have to wear nappies when I am on home detention."

"Mums can be pretty tough, but as I am one myself, I understand. I suggest you put up with the nappies and make the best of the year ahead."

"I will."

"I also noticed you sitting very uncomfortably as well. I know *that* behaviour as well."

Sophie looked at him for reaction, but there wasn't one.

"Your mum smacked you today, didn't she?"

He nodded.

The making of a baby

"Seems like she is trying to set you on the straight and narrow, so good for her. Those elderly people you hurt are going to suffer for a long time. You will only suffer for a year. When your mum smacks you next time, remember you probably deserved it."

"Yes, Sophie," he whispered.

"Your mum I are both trying to make you into a better person, so do as you are told at home and then you and I will never have to deal with each other again, once your year is up."

"I will, I promise."

"And I am sure you will learn too. Say hi to your mum from me on the way out and I will see you in a month's time. Or when you suddenly find me at your front door!"

"I will. Thank you."

Jordan was quiet in the car on the way home, still thinking about what had just happened. Even though it was less than a week of detention, being out of the house and grounds seemed like a holiday. He wanted to go and get a burger, but he had been warned that trips to the parole officer were to be by the most direct route and with no stops. He was after all, still effectively in a prison, even if it was in his own home.

"How did it go?" Claire asked finally.

"It was okay."

"That's all he had to say?"

"It's a she, mum. Sophie."

"What did she have to say then?"

"She could tell I was wearing a nappy!" he exclaimed unhappily. "And she could even tell you spanked me this morning!"

"She is probably trained to notice these things," Claire replied, not at all sure that it was the truth. "But it doesn't matter, because we are back home now."

The making of a baby

The Jaguar XJ cruised through the gate and parked under the large carport at the side of the house. Jordan was stressed and unhappy. Even though Sophie was nice to him, she was also very firm and a bit threatening.

Everyone's telling me what I can do and can't do. And mum is spanking me again and it's all a bit too hard. I just want this to be over.

They were inside only five minutes when a delivery truck arrived at the front of the house. As Jordan watched, he saw two men carry a thickly plastic-wrapped piece of furniture down the hall.

"Can you put it in here please?" said Claire and the two men carried the odd item into the nursery. "Thank you!"

After they left the house, Jordan walked into the nursery and saw his mother unwrapping something that looked familiar and yet, not.

"It's a changing table, Jordan!" she announced with a flourish.

His face fell. It was a nappy-changing table.

"Changing you on your bed is hard on my back, so I ordered this changing table to make it easier on us both. You can climb up on here and I can change your nappies so much easier!"

Claire was excited. Jordan however, was not that thrilled.

The wooden adult-size change table was painted in glossy white and pink and the tabletop was covered in nursery-print vinyl. It was easily wiped down for any accidents from nappy changes.

There were three cupboards underneath and Jordan watched in dismay, as his mother packed his nappies and plastic pants in there along with his pins, baby powder and cream. He was even more embarrassed to see not one, but three dummies.

"Are you wet yet?" asked Claire enthusiastically. She wanted to try out her new nursery furniture.

Without waiting for him to answer, she put her hand inside his plastic pants before withdrawing them with a disappointed look.

The making of a baby

"Still only damp. I think you have another hour or so. I will change you after lunch."

True to her word, two hours later, an embarrassed Jordan pulled his shoes and trousers off and stepped up to the brand-new adult nappy change table and laid down.

"This is much easier on mummy," she said. "No more bending and lifting on here. Now lift your legs for mummy," she asked.

Jordan lifted his legs and revealed his deep red backside, still stinging from two spankings in two days.

"Let me put some cream on this for you, baby," she said and reached into the cupboard below to retrieve some cream and slathered it all over his sore backside. "You won't disobey me again, will you, baby?"

"No mum... mum... mummy," he replied, tripping over his words.

Claire smiled at him, thrilled that 'mummy' was making a comeback again, if only hesitantly.

"Would you like to go for a walk in the garden with me again, baby?" she asked, as she expertly pinned a new nappy onto him and slid up his plastic pants.

"Yes, mummy. It was fun yesterday."

"Well your pants are too tight to be comfortable, so I have something that is perhaps a bit better for you. Get down from the change table and I will get it for you."

Jordan stepped down as his mother returned from the nursery cupboard holding an odd kind of long t-shirt.

"Arms up, baby," she asked and pulled the pastel pink with blue edging 'shirt' over his head and down his body. She then reached down and pulled the back part of the 'shirt' between his nappied legs and with five press studs, connected the two pieces

The making of a baby

"It's a onesie, baby!" Claire explained. "When you wear a nappy, you need a special shirt to hold the nappy up and cover you properly. So, while you are wearing nappies, you can wear this as well. I think you will find it very comfortable."

Jordan looked at the obviously babyish item of clothing and was about to complain when his bottom reminded him forcefully that a third spanking might really hurt.

"Thanks, mummy," he said. "It's very nice."

"I know my boy likes pink, so I got you a pink one!"

Jordan smiled. Ever since the fiasco of the *Great Panty Incident* many years ago, his mother had made several attempts to understand it, but to no avail. Now she was just putting pink into his life and rolling with it.

Claire took some ribbon, tied it to his rejected pink dummy and pinned it to his onesie.

"You don't have to use it, baby," she explained. "But if you need your dummy, it will always be there for you."

It made no sense to him at all, but he didn't complain or even comment about it.

Claire took hold of his hand and once again, they walked through the garden with Jordan in just his nappy and onesie and some sandals. This time, he held onto her hand tightly.

"You know what this garden needs?" said Claire. "I think it needs a sandpit and maybe, even a swing set. What do you think?"

Before he even had time to think through his answer, he replied. "Oh, mummy, that would be great!"

Jordan had loved the swings as a child and hated getting 'too old' to play on them anymore. Only a year earlier he had taken a detour on his way home from school and spent ten minutes playing on the swings, wishing he was still young enough to do it all the time.

"Well, I think I will get some swings put in so you can play while you are stuck here. And what about a sandpit? Would you like one of those too?"

"Yes."

"Er, yes what?" she asked.

"Yes, please?" he offered.

"Yes, please who?"

"Yes, please, mummy!" he said and smiled broadly, squeezing her hand.

"I love you, baby. I love you so much, little boy!"

"I love you too, mummy," he said and then he hugged her.

They walked around the garden for a while longer, holding hands and talking about the things they liked. They were just by the back door when Claire turned around and faced her son.

"I need to ask you something I should have a lot of years ago. Jordan, do you want to be a girl?"

He was silent for a while before he burst into tears.

"I don't know, mummy!" he sobbed for the second time that day. "Sometimes I think I do and other times I don't, and I don't know how I feel."

Claire hugged him to herself.

"It's okay my precious little baby. You can be a girl or a boy if you want or both. I just don't want you to be unhappy."

Claire took his pinned-on dummy and placed it in his mouth and he gratefully sucked on it while his mother wiped his tears away.

"I think someone needs a nap," she said.

A few minutes later, Jordan was in his bed, happily sucking his dummy and slowly falling asleep.

My little girl?

C laire leaned over the awakening child

"Wakey, Wakey, little baby," she said. "Time to get up. My, you sleep a lot now you are in nappies, don't you?"

"Mummy, how long will I be in nappies?"

There was no anger, no rancour or unhappiness. He simply wanted to know the answer.

"Well, my little girl..."

The making of a baby

Claire looked at his face and saw the smile that erupted at calling him a girl.

"You still wet the bed and I've noticed you can't stay dry during the day either, can you?"

"I don't understand, mummy," he said. "I used to be able to stay dry during the day before, but now I can't!"

"Sometimes things change, dear. You went through something very traumatic in court and it can affect people sometimes. You need to trust mummy that I love you and know what is best for you. Can you do that?"

"Yes mummy, I trust you."

"Good girl, now one thing that has changed is that you need to be in nappies now and maybe for a long time. They keep you dry and clean and safe. That is something you don't need to worry about, and I can help you with everything."

Jordan popped his dummy back in his mouth, as he got up from his bed.

"I'm going to play Legos for a while, mummy," he said around the dummy.

"Okay dear," she replied. "Have fun."

Claire sat in the living room, holding the book that was guiding her actions. The author, Amanda Marsden, had chosen to protect her son from the horrors of war in her own special and unusual way, and it had worked. Her son had also been a bedwetter for a long time, although, unlike Jordan, he hadn't reverted back to it. But it was an easy task just the same to get him back into nappies and Claire had also found that getting *her* son back into nappies had been far easier than she had expected. It might have required two fairly harsh spankings, but she had achieved it, nonetheless.

"I guess what helps is that nappies are also a practical advantage for him during the night, so he doesn't have wet sheets and that part was easy," she thought to herself. "Daytimes took some convincing, but I am surprised how in only a little while, he has accepted nappies during the day. Amanda was sure right about that in her book!"

She read the passage once more.

"Boys that have wet the bed past the age of twelve are easy targets for returning to nappies. For most of them, a return to bedwetting is never far away. They may have ceased actual wet sheets, but to have stayed wet for so long indicates that it would not be difficult to return them to it again. Nappies are the solution to that. Wet sheets are an uncomfortable impediment to boys reverting to bedwetting, but a warm cosy nappy makes it so much easier. There is no discomfort, there is no middle of the night bathroom trips and there is no fear of a wet bed. If you can get your boy back into night nappies, wetting them will take very little time at all. Just deny them toilet access before bedtime and during the night and nature will take care of the rest.

Day nappies are more complex and will take a little more time, but the same principle applies. A lot of the reasons that boys wet the bed for so long is that they are not fully suited to toilet training and it is a poor fit for them. They manage it during the day when they can be on guard, but during sleep, they wet the bed. By putting them in day nappies, they no longer have to worry about dryness at all and beginning to wet their day nappies is a very natural step for them. Keep them in day nappies just a few days and they will be wetting without awareness very easily."

Claire had seen exactly that take place with Jordan. His bedwetting was very long-lasting and had only barely stopped when it started up again after the death of his father and it had never stopped since. Not a single dry night. She had been equally astonished how she had not needed to ban Jordan from the toilet during the day. In fact, when she checked his nappy every few hours, it was always wet, and he was wetting without much – if any – conscious control.

Her reverie was broken by the arrival of Connie, home from work a little earlier than expected.

"Have you seen Jordan in the nursery?" she exclaimed, a look of surprise covering her face. "He's sucking on his dummy like there's no tomorrow!"

"I know!" Claire responded. "And he seems so much happier and behaved with it."

"How did you ever get him to use it?"

"He was really tired last night, and I popped it in, and he took to it very easily."

"But I saw you spank him this morning for throwing it away, so what gives now?"

"It was more than just his dummy. He was being rebellious and disobedient about everything. You probably shouldn't have been there for that."

"It was fun to watch though!" she smirked. "I'm glad it wasn't me!"

"Well, you know that we both decided we had to get him on the straight and narrow and that is part of it. He has to learn to obey and do as he is told."

"Is he going to wear nappies for long?" she asked.

Claire smirked. "I don't have any plans for him to ever be out of them. I don't think he is even capable of it. By the way, did you see the new change table I ordered? It arrived today. It is simply beautiful."

"No, I missed it. I didn't want him to see me watching him. He is still playing with his Legos."

"I need to change his nappy soon and you can take a look at it then."

Claire went to a folded over section of the book about starting boys on a dummy.

"A dummy is a truly essential element of restoring infantile balance to boys. Once they are safely in nappies, it is time to give them a dummy, but you need to be clever about how you do it. If you just shove a dummy in his mouth at any old time, he will spit it out and it will be even harder next time.

If he is deeply asleep, you can try to insert it into his mouth and jiggle it around until he is aware of it and begins to suck on it. Until he actively sucks, he hasn't really accepted it. You may need to try several times until the sucking commences. Also, if your boy is crying or deeply distressed, this is a perfect time to give him a dummy. The other time is what we have talked about before – his baby impulses. All boys have moments of acting like babies, something that never really goes away, but for your special boy, there will be times when he will slip into a mode that is more babyish or infantile than usual and, it will look authentic. It isn't easily possible to explain this, but when you see it, you will recognise it. Your boy will take the dummy with relative ease. He may still object some, but if you insist, he will take it and once he starts sucking it, you have a boy who will use a dummy from then on. You might need to keep pushing for a while, but before long, he won't be able to sleep without one and you will need to have one with you all the time, in case he needs it during the day. Ideally, your boy will have a dummy pinned to his clothes all the time and have it in his mouth more often than not.

Babies are very oral and so, a dummy is an important tool for them. Many boys grow up with that same oral fixation. Ideally, you never take a dummy away at all, but in the real world, you are going to have to reintroduce it to him. Once he has embraced the oral fixation that only a dummy can satisfy, you are ready to move on to bigger and better things.

A boy that will take the teat of a dummy, is only steps away from the teat of a bottle or breast. Keep that in mind as you train him with a dummy. It is a key step and not one to skip over."

"Connie, Jordan needs a nappy change. If he is not too self-conscious, you can stay, but if I ask you to leave, do it without complaint, okay?"

As the two women stepped into the nursery, Connie spied the magnificent changing table.

"Mum, that is brilliant!" she exclaimed. "How did you get it to match the colours in the nursery?"

"It wasn't an accident," she replied, cryptically. "Jordan dear, it is time for your nappy change. Connie is here too."

"Hi, sis! I didn't see you. I'm building Legos."

Connie was speechless. Jordan was sitting in his pink onesie and answered her without taking his dummy out.

"He's a child!" she whispered to her mother.

"I know," she whispered back. "Try not to spook him."

Jordan stood up and went to the change table. He wasn't at all self-conscious as Claire undid the clasps on his onesie and pulled down his plastic pants.

"Up on the table, little girl," she said.

"Little girl?" Connie mouthed wordlessly to her mother.

Claire unpinned the sodden nappy and dropped it in the nappy bucket nearby.

"Connie, can you fold a nappy for your brother, please? I forgot to do it before I got him up here."

"I don't know how, mum," she replied.

"Let me show you how. You are going to need to know how to do this."

Connie's eyes widened as she understood exactly what her mother was saying. She watched the steps of taking the large

The making of a baby

towelling square and folding it in a kite shape and then into a well - proportioned nappy, suited to Jordan's size.

Claire then slipped the nappy under Jordan's bottom, taking extra notice of his still very red and sore bottom and double-pinned both sides.

"You should fold the nappy *before* you change baby, so don't forget. It's a lot harder to fold it on the floor!"

"The plastic pants are on the left of the first cupboard. Can you get me some please?"

Connie grabbed a pair of pink plastic pants and with her mother helping, slid them up Jordan's legs. Claire showed her how to ensure the entire nappy was covered and protected.

"There we go, baby!" exclaimed Claire. "All changed. Connie, can you clip his onesie back together for him, please?"

Connie nervously pulled the two parts of his onesie together and pressed the five studs together.

"Dinner is in just ten minutes, baby. You can play for ten minutes and then it is dinner time. After that, it is bath time."

"Mum," Connie asked after they left the nursery. "Why did you make me help you?"

"Constance," her mother said, using her full name. "We both agreed to do whatever was necessary to pull him back into line, remember?"

"I know, but – "

"No buts about it. I will need you to change his nappies sometimes and to help out with bathing and dressing and whatever comes up next."

"I don't want to," she complained. "But I'll do it to keep stinky out of jail. But what's with calling him a girl?"

"I don't know yet. That's new today. He loves girl's things and when I called him a girl, he went all weak at the knees. We'll see where this goes over time."

Jordan sat happily at dinner, with his dummy hanging on the end of the ribbon. He told his sister about going to the parole officer and how nice she was. He also told her about the garden and what he wanted to do there.

Connie was perplexed by what she was seeing. Firstly, her brother was being polite and not rude, but he was also sharing about himself and even asking her about her day. If not for the thick nappy and dummy hanging from his pink onesie, he would have looked and sounded like any other polite young man. Connie found it weird. She was more used to rudeness, sullenness and sadly, the appearance of cops at the door to inform them he had been arrested. It was a definite improvement.

"Bath time, baby!" announced Claire.

"Excellent!" exclaimed Jordan excitedly.

"Let me go and run it for you, baby. Just stay here until I call you. Connie, would you bring him to the bathroom when I call?"

Claire left the room.

"Stinky!" she whispered. "What are you doing? You're acting like a baby!"

"No, I'm not!" he retorted.

"You're wearing nappies and wetting them!"

"I need them, sis. I can't go without them!"

"What about the dummy? What about that?"

"I dunno..." he replied, sounding unsure about it as well. "It just feels nice and no one can see me, so why does it matter?"

"Well if you're happy then. Oh, by the way, I watched you get the paddle this morning. You cried like a little girl!"

Jordan blushed and began to tear up a tiny bit.

"Oh, sorry stinky. I didn't mean anything. But I warned you mum had it."

"I'm trying to do the best, but I don't understand how to do things and how I feel."

"About what things?"

"Everything and about girl things too." Jordan looked down at the table.

"Jordan! Connie! The bath is ready!" Claire called out from the bathroom down the hall.

"It's Saturday tomorrow," said Connie. "Would you like me to show you about being a girl?"

"If mum lets me, sure!"

"I'll ask her, stinky. Now, mum wants you in the bath."

When they entered the bathroom, they could see the tub filled with bubbles.

"I thought you might like a bubble bath tonight, baby."

Jordan answered by immediately lifting his arms so his mother could remove his onesie.

The nappy was barely damp and came off easily and he stepped into the bath with a broad smile and not a single moment of self-conscious hesitation.

The bath was a lot of fun for Jordan, more fun than he could recall. Connie invited herself in for a few minutes to watch him play and was very surprised to see just how much he enjoyed it. He played with the bubbles and squeezed the bath toys, smiling and grinning the whole time.

"I haven't seen him this happy for years, mum!" Connie told her mum after she left him in the bath.

The making of a baby

"I know!" Claire replied. "It is amazing. He was so angry and sullen and…"

"A pain in the arse?" Connie suggested.

"And that too!" her mother laughed. "But I just want to make sure he stays this way."

Mother and daughter had previously had a long discussion on Jordan and what to do about him after his arrest and court appearance. Claire had told Connie about the upcoming home detention and that she was going to use the year to 'fix' him before he was able to go back into the world.

"Connie, we need to have a talk about Jordan and what's about to happen," said Claire. They were sitting in the comfortable lounge room of their up-market, inner-city home.

"I just got off the phone from one of my friends and she informed me that Jordan is going to get home detention and not jail."

"Phew!" exhaled Connie. "That's great!"

"Yes, I know," sighed Claire. "I pulled all the strings I could, but while Jordan is with his lawyer, I need to talk to you about what happens next."

"I'm glad he won't be going to jail," Connie said, her voice showing her relief. "He might be a stinky sod, but he would not do well in jail, especially with his bedwetting."

"Well, it seems like his bedwetting is the thing that convinced the Magistrate to give him home detention. I don't know how long yet, but my friend thinks somewhere between nine and eighteen months."

"All that time stuck in here. He will go bat-shit crazy!"

The making of a baby

"That's what I wanted to talk to you about. I've bought a new house."

Claire described the new home to her daughter, who eventually came around to the idea. The drive to her job was longer, but not that much further.

"But the house is just part of it. I want to fix Jordan up."

"Fix him up?"

"I've been seeing this for a few years now and his arrest just forced me to face the fact that he is a bit broken. And his bedwetting is a bit of a clue."

"How is bedwetting a clue?"

"I've been reading a book about correcting the behaviour of wayward boys and teens and one of the things it says is that bedwetting in teens without medical reasons is a sign that they haven't grown up properly. Let me ask you this. Have you ever heard Jordan complain about his bedwetting?"

"No, not really, he just gets up in his stinky panties and doesn't seem to care one way or the other."

"Exactly!" Claire exclaimed. "He doesn't care that he wets the bed or that you and I know about it. I think he parades in his wet panties to remind us of it. And he never changes his wet sheets. If I don't do it, it doesn't happen."

"So, what are you saying?"

"I am saying that Jordan is still a child in many ways and if I am going to fix him, I need to fix the child first."

"Yeah okay, I kind of get that, but how do you fix the child when he is an adult now?"

"The book says you start by putting him back into nappies for his bedwetting and during the day as well."

Connie looked at her mother in shock.

The making of a baby

"Good luck on getting him to do that!" she spat out. "You can't even get him to clean his room and you want him to start wearing nappies again?"

"You seem to forget that he will be on parole and unable to leave the house. He will have to do as I say!"

"And this *book* of yours says that putting him in nappies will fix all the shit he does?"

"It's more than that. But it's a start. But I am telling you this because I will need your help to support me. There will be a lot of things that will happen, and I need you to be on my side and sometimes, my helper."

"Okay," she replied, feeling less than convinced. "I'll help you where I can, but I guess no more stinky wet beds and panties would be an improvement around here! I just don't know about the nappies thing though."

Connie remembered that conversation from only a few weeks ago when she asked her mother about the following day's proposed feminine adventure.

"Mum, I asked Jordan if he wanted me to help him explore a bit of femininity tomorrow. Is that okay?"

Claire smiled. "I think that is a great idea and your timing is perfect. I need to go into the city for four or five hours tomorrow and I can't leave him alone and wondered if you would babysit him?"

"Babysit?" she gulped. She instantly knew what that meant.

"Yes, remember when you promised to do whatever was needed to help me fix your brother?"

The making of a baby

Connie remembered only too well.

"Well, it means I will need you to change his lunchtime nappy because I won't be here, and he is not allowed to do it himself."

Connie sighed. "I don't really know how to do it and he isn't going to let me change him anyhow!"

"Then how about you get some practice right now and I will help you put on his night nappy?"

Connie gulped and then sighed. "Okay mum, but if I stab him with nappy pins, it is your fault!"

"Fold the nappy first on the change table," explained Claire, directing her daughter to the table while Jordan stood by, wrapped in just a towel. "Now Jordan, drop the towel and get up on the change table please."

The moment the towel dropped, Connie slammed her eyes shut.

"Connie, you will need your eyes open if you are going to do this!"

Connie reluctantly opened her eyes and saw her brother stark naked lying on the change table on top of the nappy she had just folded. As she approached, he automatically lifted his legs, exposing his very red bottom.

"Now since he is just out of the bath, you don't need to use baby wipes, but he does need baby powder, so shake some of that out."

Trying desperately not to look at anything, Connie shook the baby powder and it sprinkled all over him.

"Now grab the centre part of the nappy and pull it up over him."

"You mean up over his junk!" she thought, miserably.

"Now grab the side panel and bring it up and slide the corner under the front panel. Then slide a pin through it."

Connie did as instructed, trying as hard as possible not to *touch* anything. Jordan laid there smirking and enjoying her discomfort.

"Now do the other side the same way."

She pinned the other side. Claire checked her work.

"It's a bit loose, Connie," she said. "His nappy needs to be tight, so just repin the left side again."

Feeling ridiculous, Connie tightened the nappy and repinned the left side.

"Much better. Now we put another pair of pins just above the leg holes to keep them firm and we are done!"

The hard part was done, and she slipped a pair of plastic pants on and sighed deeply with relief.

"Well done, Connie!" her mother said.

"Thanks, sis!" exclaimed Jordan. He was smiling. Although being nappied by his sister was no great experience, he had enjoyed her very obvious discomfort.

"Now, let's get you in your pyjamas and ready for bed!" Claire added.

Ten minutes later, Jordan was tucked up tight in his bed, sucking on his dummy and ready for a night of deep sleep.

Caitlyn

"I'm about to get going now," exclaimed Claire to her two children. "Have a good day and Jordan, obey your sister and Connie, remember what you need to do!"

Connie looked at her mother with a sense of deep resignation. She was now committed to a solo nappy change that lunchtime. Jordan was standing in Connie's bedroom wearing just his nappy and plastic pants and a pair of panties over the top.

"I think a bra should be the first thing!" Connie announced. "I know you've been wanting one for a while now."

She took a pink lacy padded bra and carefully put it on Jordan.

"If you are going to wear a bra all the time, you will have to learn how to put one on yourself."

"I don't think mummy will let me have one yet," said Jordan.

"One day perhaps, but for today I think we need to pad out these boobies of yours since you have… nothing!"

Connie rolled up some short socks and filled out Jordan's bra.

"Look at those legs!" exclaimed Connie in mock horror. "We definitely need to shave them. Come into the bathroom and I will show you how to shave your own legs."

The two siblings giggled as Jordan shaved his legs for the first time, leaving a few nicks along the way. It took quite a while. He was quite hairy.

"That's better!" Connie declared. "And now it is time to do something with those nails. Come into the kitchen and let's make you pretty!"

Despite the upcoming threat of a nappy change, Connie was enjoying herself. She carefully applied two coats of soft pink nail polish to his toenails and fingernails.

"Now you have to sit very still while they dry, Jordan," she explained. "But while you sit there, I will see if there is anything I can do with your hair."

Jordan's hair was longish, but not long enough to do much with.

"Are you going to grow it longer like a girl?" Connie asked.

"If mummy lets me," he replied.

"I've got to ask, what's with calling her 'mummy' all of a sudden?"

Jordan shrugged. "It just seems right, you know?"

"Okay," she sighed. "Whatever you want. I can't do much with your hair, but how about some makeup?"

Jordan's eyes lit up. "Yes, please!"

For the next hour, Connie applied foundation, eyeshadow, mascara, and lipstick.

"You look really pretty, Jordan," she said. "I didn't realise before, but with a bit of help, you really do look like a girl."

"Thanks, sis," he replied. "I think I've wanted to be a girl for a while."

"I have wondered about that. The whole panty thing did sort of beg that question. How sure are you that you want to be a girl?"

"I'm not completely sure, but I've been considering it for a few years now and I do think I want to be a girl."

"A girl or a baby girl?" she asked. "Because that nappy of yours is pretty obvious and to be honest, you don't seem to be complaining about it much."

"I don't know. Mummy seems pretty determined for me to have a dummy. And the nappy and dummy do feel kind of right, you know?"

"Well, don't use your dummy now or you'll mess up your lipstick. I wish your ears were pierced and I could give you some very pretty earrings."

"I'm not allowed to go out and get it done," he said forlornly. "Otherwise I would."

"You know what?" suggested Connie. "I have a friend that does ear piercing and she could come here and do it for you!"

"Do you think mummy would let me?"

"We can only ask!"

Jordan stood in front of the bathroom mirror admiring his makeup and nails. He grinned constantly. He also flooded his nappy without being aware of it.

"Now it's time for you to get dressed up and show off those legs and boobs!"

Over the next hour, the two 'girls' tried on most of Connie's tops and skirts, including a pretty camisole that was kept for special occasions. Dressing up her brother, was one such 'special occasion'.

Finally, a combination of skirt and top was decided on and Jordan was finally dressed as a girl for the first time in his life.

"What do you think?" asked Connie, admiring her work.

"I feel wonderful!" exclaimed Jordan. "Thanks so much, sis!"

"There is still one thing missing," she said.

"What's that?"

"Your name. I can't look at you and call you Jordan. It's just wrong. You wear panties all the time. You wear nappies with girls' plastic pants and you even have girls' pyjamas. And now you are in girls' clothes. You need to have a girl's name."

Jordan's eyes glistened and he said nothing.

"You have a girl's name already, don't you?"

He nodded. "Caitlyn."

"That's so pretty, Caitlyn," Connie replied, momentarily overcome with the emotion of the moment. "When did you first call yourself that?"

"When I was at Kindergarten," Caitlyn replied.

"That long? Wow. Does mum know?"

She shook her head.

"I think it is time she knew, don't you?"

"Yeah, it's time," Caitlyn replied. "I'm sick of hiding it."

"Is your nappy wet?" Connie asked reluctantly.

"I don't know."

"How can you not know?" she replied, in a voice tinged with exasperation. Following her mother's example, she put two fingers underneath the back of Caitlyn's plastic pants.

"You're soaked!" she exclaimed. "And mum won't be home for a couple of hours yet, so I suppose I'll have to change you."

"Sorry sis, I'm not allowed to change myself."

"It's okay, Caitlyn," she replied. "I've changed plenty of nappies in my time, just not any this big!"

Taking charge of the situation, Connie took her newly-found sister to the nursery and took down her skirt and panties before taking a deep breath and sliding the wet plastic panties down her legs.

"Up on the table now," she said, remembering the instructions on how to change the nappy of a five-foot, six-inch, baby girl.

She unpinned the sodden nappy and dropped it into the bin. She got out the wipes and quickly wiped her bottom, daring not to go any further and then slid the freshly folded nappy under her bottom again.

"You know Caitlyn, this is actually a lot easier knowing you are a girl. Dumb, I know, but it is, just the same."

Caitlyn smiled as her sister completed the nappy change and helped her back on with the skirt.

The freshly nappy-changed girl giggled constantly during lunch while Connie sat back and admired her handiwork and the feeling that she had just let out a girl that had been trapped inside for many years.

"Let's go outside!" suggested Connie, and the two new sisters walked outside and sat on the chairs in the sun. It was still a bit cool, so Connie found a pretty, knitted cardigan for Caitlyn to wear over the top.

After a while, Caitlyn began to fidget and play with her mouth.

"Caitlyn," asked Connie. "Do you need your dummy?"

She nodded.

"Stay there and I will go and get it for you."

A few minutes later, Connie knelt next to her new sister, pinned the dummy ribbon to her top and slipped it into her welcoming mouth. Then she handed her a pink teddy bear.

"Caitlyn, this is Jenny. She has been my teddy bear since I was twelve and I think she needs a new friend to be with her. Can you be her new friend?"

Connie had seen what her mother had seen the day before. Adult Caitlyn had gone, and baby Caitlyn had arrived. Sucking on her dummy, she cuddled Jenny like a long-lost friend.

It was also clearly time for a nap. This was not part of the plan.

"I think it is time for a nap, Caitlyn," Connie suggested softly.

She took hold of her sister's hand and gently led her inside to her bedroom. She took off the skirt and top but left the bra on, so as to not distract her. She carefully put on her pyjama top and laid her back on the bed. Pulling back the sheet and quilt, she kissed Caitlyn on the forehead and turned the light out as she left.

In her bedroom, she softly wept, as she recalled the voice of both her adult sister and now the look of her infant sister. She understood what her mother had been saying all along. Her brother... no her sister... was broken and needed their support and help. And she was now in on the plan, one hundred per cent.

"How'd it go?" asked Claire, the moment she stepped through the front door.

"Shh! Caitlyn is asleep!"

The making of a baby

Claire stared at her for a moment. "Caitlyn?"

"Jordan's name is Caitlyn and he has wanted to use it since he was like, four years old!"

Connie briefly told her what had happened during the day and how she had dressed Caitlyn up fully and also, how she had slipped back to being a young child when sitting outside.

"You didn't put her down without changing her nappy, did you?" asked Claire, afraid of the wet mess that might occur.

"No mum. I changed her before and no, I didn't freak out and I even kept my eyes open!"

Claire laughed.

"You know, it's a lot easier changing a girl than a boy! Serious!"

The idiocy of the statement made perfect sense to both women. Claire had suspected that apart from the first couple of angst-ridden nappy changes, she had actually been changing a girl. Now, she knew she was correct. Together they cracked open the door of Caitlyn's bedroom and peered in.

"She looks like an angel there, cuddling her teddy bear," whispered Claire. "What made you give it to her?"

"I needed Jenny to sleep with me for a few years, and I can see now that she really needs her more than I do."

"She might need a few teddy bears, I think," commented her mother.

It was only thirty minutes later that Caitlyn stirred awake.

"Mummy!" she called out. "Can I get up please?"

Claire came in immediately. She had been waiting for her to wake up.

"Hello sweetheart!" she exclaimed. "Did you have a good sleep?"

The making of a baby

Caitlyn's dummy was hanging from the ribbon pinned to her pyjamas.

"Yes, mummy."

"Your sister tells me your name is Caitlyn, is that right?"

She nodded and Claire could tell that the adult had returned, but not the boy.

"Yes, I chose that name when I was four but didn't tell anyone."

"Well, from now on, we will call you Caitlyn and you are one of us girls!"

"Thanks, mum!" she exclaimed.

Inwardly, Claire was disappointed it was back to 'mum' instead of 'mummy', but the question of gender was at least, now resolved.

"Now I have a surprise for you, and this is why I was in the city this morning. How about you come to my bedroom and I will show it to you!"

The three of them went into Claire's room. There on the bed lay a baby girl's dress in pink with white lace and satin collar. It was beautiful.

"This is for you, Caitlyn. I was waiting until you told me you were a girl and now you have, it is yours to wear."

"Mummy, can I put it on?"

"Sure thing, sweetheart, but we will need to take off your bra for now. Maybe when you are a bit older you can start wearing a bra all the time."

Connie helped take off her pyjama top and bra.

"You should wear a onesie with this, Caitlyn," she suggested. "It will keep you fresh and clean and help hold your nappy up."

Claire quickly pulled a plain white onesie on and fastened it together underneath her nappy. Then, she took the pink dress and

slipped it over Caitlyn's head and did up the buttons at the back. The dress was clearly meant for someone who had a mummy to help them put it on.

"And now the frilly nappy cover!"

Caitlyn pulled up the frilly white and pink lace-trimmed pants designed to go over a bulky nappy.

"Wow!" exclaimed Connie. "You look fabulous!"

"And there's something else you need," said Claire as she revealed a pair of pink Crocs in Caitlyn's size.

"You can't go outside without shoes, little girl, so I got something a bit more girly and a bit more your age," she said diplomatically. She had wanted to say, 'more babyish', but didn't want to spoil the mood.

Caitlyn excitedly pulled on the shoes.

"They almost match your nail polish," Claire commented. "Well done with that, by the way!"

"Mummy, can I go outside, please?" Caitlyn begged.

"It's a bit cool outside and I think you need something on your head."

From another parcel on the bed, Claire pulled out an exquisite white and pink broderie Anglaise baby bonnet in her size. It was trimmed with white lace. Caitlyn grinned from ear to ear as her mother put the classic baby bonnet on her head and tied the ribbons together. The child was back.

"Now we can all go outside!" announced Claire.

Connie and her mother took one hand each of their newly-discovered baby girl and walked across the lawn together. Caitlyn enjoyed her new clothes and the experience of being just who she was. Finally. For part of the journey around the various garden paths, the little girl could only hold one other person's hand and so she

alternated between her mother and her sister. The dummy rarely left her mouth.

Connie eventually tired of the gardens and returned back inside.

"I love you, mummy," said Caitlyn, from behind her dummy.

"I said we would help you find yourself and I think we are doing that now, don't you agree?"

She nodded and grabbed for her mother's hand again.

"When are we getting swings, mummy?"

Claire smiled.

"I actually bought a set of swings and a slippery dip today and they will be delivered tomorrow or the day after."

"Yay!" exclaimed a very happy little girl.

Suddenly Caitlyn stopped walking and held her tummy.

"What's wrong, sweetheart?" asked her mother.

"Mummy, I need to do a poo!"

"That's okay, Caitlyn," she answered. "You are wearing a nappy, so just do it in there. No need to feel bad about it."

"I don't know…"

Claire hugged her little girl.

"It's all okay, sweetheart. Everything is fine. You can just do it in your nappy anytime. You don't need a toilet. You are still a bit too little for that. Just push into your nappy, there's a good girl."

Claire broke the hug and put her hand on Caitlyn's tummy and pushed lightly.

"It's time to do it now, sweetheart. Let it all go. Poo into your nappy and mummy will take care of it."

Caitlyn locked eyes with her mother and relaxed. Immediately, her bowels opened and she emptied into her nappy with little effort.

"Well done, little girl! Well done, Caitlyn! Mummy's proud of you. Now we can continue our walk."

The two continued walking hand in hand until they came to a little stone seat near the rear fence. Claire sat down and motioned her reluctant daughter to sit down with her. As Caitlyn sat down, she felt the two days' worth of mess spread beneath her. It was surprisingly, *not* uncomfortable.

"I can change you once we get back inside, honey. But there's no rush. It is just you and me out here with the wind and the sun and the pretty garden."

Claire smiled deeply as her now-smelly daughter leant up against her and relaxed.

"We are mother and baby once more," she thought, deep inside her soul.

Sophie's Decision

For the next three weeks, the Airesdale household experienced a sense of peace it had not had during the years of Jordan's misbehaviour, arguing and finally arrest. It was a bizarre sense of calm that was a welcome change.

Caitlyn had appeared and Jordan was as yet still unsighted. At times, Caitlyn was a teenage girl and at other times, a young child. At all times, however, she was in a nappy and since that first fateful soiling experience, had relinquished control and used her nappy fully. It was a pivotal moment for Caitlyn's restoration.

Claire often re-read the passage from her book that referred to what had taken place that day.

"Deep inside all of us is a deep reluctance to soil ourselves. It is not really surprising, is it? We can have 'accidents' and leak pee into our underwear and it is mildly embarrassing, but not greatly so. We can even be bedwetters and awake every morning to a sizable wet patch beneath us and while it is perhaps humiliating, it is not that hard to hide and we can still maintain our adultness with ease.

You can put your wayward son back into nappies and wetting them is not difficult to do. The barrier to getting him to wet his nappy is not terribly high and if he was already a bedwetter, it is one that is easily scaled. Wet days are a short journey from wet nights.

The wet nappy is a relatively small step, but the dirty nappy is not.

Dirtying the nappy means discarding every pretence we have, both for you the parent and for the boy you are helping. It means that we no longer have control anymore. It also distinguishes between child and baby. A young child might still wear nappies, but most do not poo in them. A toilet-training routine first stops the pooing in nappies. The peeing comes later. But a baby... a baby poos in their nappy.

When your son has his first dirty nappy, it is a sign that he is moving back towards babyhood and infancy. Losing effective bladder control is not that hard when your boy is in nappies all the time and for a bedwetter, easier still. A nappy is a convenience, an easy alternative to the toilet that adults and older children use. But a dirty nappy is not a convenience. It is smelly and can be uncomfortable for an older child. But to a baby, it IS a convenience, a natural way to eliminate, anywhere and anytime.

Achieving the first dirty nappy is a big step. Having more of them, however, is an even bigger one. You must make a big deal out of the first dirty nappy and congratulate them and if possible, reward them. Make it known that you expect and want continual dirty nappies and that you are willing to change them without complaint.

The making of a baby

No, changing dirty nappies is not fun, but what they mean is worth the inconvenience. Once they are dirtying their nappies consistently, you have effectively told them that they are babies to some degree and they are forced to agree, however reluctantly. You have changed their direction.

Don't rush to change them if possible. Letting them sit in their dirty nappy for thirty minutes to an hour does them good. It helps them accept the inevitability of the situation and helps to normalise it. You want wet and dirty nappies to be <u>normal</u>, because to a baby, they <u>are</u> normal."

Caitlyn had embraced her dummy and it was pinned to every outfit she wore, day and night and it spent at least half of the day in her mouth. Claire had bought her several more baby dresses and onesies so that she was never in her unwanted male clothes anymore. Another pair of very infantile style pyjamas was added to her selection. Pretty bonnets were worn whenever she went outside and often inside as well.

Claire took the bulk of the nappy changes, including all the dirty ones. Connie was a reluctant nappy changer and dirty ones involved too much 'intimate contact' for her to cope with. But she maintained Caitlyn's nails and true to her word, arranged for a friend to come and pierce her ears.

It was the only other time Caitlyn had worn Connie's clothes while her ears were getting pierced. As a present, her mother bought her some very pretty gold earrings she had worn since. And Connie added some lovely gold and diamond earrings.

Jenny the teddy bear went with Caitlyn almost everywhere. Every sleep and every nap had her in bed, tightly cuddling the teddy bear. While playing on the floor in the nursery, Jenny sat and watched. While walking around the garden with her mother as she did at least once a day, Jenny came along to keep her company.

It was not all smooth sailing. The anger that had so damaged Jordan, still lived inside the increasingly pretty girl. As her hair grew, Connie did her best to make it look as feminine as possible. On weekends when she had the time, she would do Caitlyn's makeup although, with a dummy, lipstick was a bust.

Claire imposed tight rules on Caitlyn, including not going outside on her own. Once, when she found her outside, Claire dragged her inside, pulled her wet nappy down and paddled her in the entrance hall. Another tantrum over something trivial earned her the hardest spanking she had yet received and confined to her bed for the rest of the afternoon.

However, Caitlyn was becoming a generally happier child. She was dirtying her nappy easily and more often, usually once a day. As per the book's instructions, Claire complimented and congratulated her on every dirty nappy. She was finding it easier and more natural to do. Her wet nappies were constant and uncontrolled. She often marvelled at just how easy it had been to have her wetting her nappy without control and it had only taken a few days to do so.

"Perhaps what Amanda wrote about teenage bedwetters had some truth to it. Maybe Caitlyn was never really fully toilet-trained in the first place. I guess the first accidental dirty nappy proved that," she mused one night while lying in bed. "It was just a bit *too* easy."

But it was almost a month later that the first real challenge came. It was Caitlyn's second appointment with her Parole Officer, and she would have to go as Jordan.

During her bath the night before, Claire decided to get involved in the bathing. Caitlyn needed her hair washed and had shown a less than brilliant effort beforehand doing it herself. In addition, she needed to clean off her makeup and make sure her fingernails were devoid of the pretty nail polish that Connie had applied and changed regularly.

It was only the second time Claire had directly bathed Caitlyn. The first time was after a spectacularly heavy dirty nappy that had

spread out of the nappy and hit her dress. She wasn't going to trust her to clean herself properly and had made sure every inch was scrubbed clean. She had dirtied her nappy that afternoon as well, and while clean up had been successful, she wanted her daughter to be clean and odour-free before she met the parole officer. The smell of baby powder and nappies was cute on a baby, not so much in a Corrections Office.

Dressing her in a nappy and plastic pants was routine. Putting her in trousers and a shirt, however, was not. It had been almost a month since she was last in them and to Claire's mind, she looked ridiculous. Caitlyn had not behaved well during her dressing and had earned a dozen hand slaps on the tops of her legs. She was decidedly nervous and uncomfortable about her male clothes.

The first time she had seen Caitlyn in Connie's clothes, she was stunned at just how pretty she was. Caitlyn was short for a man, but the normal height for a girl. Her build was slim and with makeup, looked very feminine. The bulkiness of her nappy took away from the fit of Connie's typically short skirts, but Claire knew that a better fitting longer skirt would hide it fairly easily. It was a long time until the end of her detention, but already she was planning a shopping expedition for away-from-home clothes for her.

In her haste to dress her for her meeting, however, Claire forgot to put on Caitlyn's white onesie. The garment would ensure that her nappy would not be exposed if she bent over.

"Jordan Airesdale!" shouted the disinterested receptionist at the Corrections Office.

Caitlyn gripped his mother's hand in fear. It was difficult the first time he had attended wearing a nappy as part of what he

The making of a baby

assumed was punishment, but now, he was wearing a nappy for genuine need and more importantly, he was now a girl and spending his entire days and nights as a girl. Being Jordan again, felt wrong. And if anything, his jeans felt like they had shrunk, and his nappy was even more obvious. He was missing the comfort of his dummy dreadfully and felt embarrassed about that as well.

"Good morning, Jordan," said Sophie cheerfully. "I trust the last month hasn't been too difficult for you?"

"No," he said. "It's been fine."

They discussed the normal things about what he had done – which was pretty much nothing – and any planned excursions.

"I see you've had your ears pierced," she observed. "Who did them for you?"

"My sister's friend does piercing and she came over to the house to do them for me."

"That's what I wanted to know. I don't want to find out you've been leaving the house and breaking your home detention."

"No, I won't do that."

"And I can see you are still in nappies. In fact, I can see them when your shirt rides up."

Caitlyn quickly pulled her shirt down to cover the exposed plastic pants.

"And looking at the way you are sitting, has mum smacked you this morning?"

"Yes, Sophie."

"I think I understand. What did you do wrong?"

Caitlyn tried to make up a credible reason for the spanking, not that she misbehaved while being dressed.

"I was rude to mummy, er... Mum," he stammered.

"And so, she smacked you for that?"

"Yeah."

"What kind of earrings do you have? Diamond ones? Gold?"

It was a trap question.

"My sister bought me some pretty diamond drop earrings and mum got me some white gold and sapphire ones."

She knew she had made a mistake the moment she stopped talking. She only had plain silver keepers in at the moment, discreet and mostly hidden by her hair.

"They sound very pretty. You are very lucky to have a mum that cares for you so much. Perhaps I should talk to your mother as well."

"No, please don't," he said, almost in a panic.

"I don't want her involved in any of this."

"Jordan, my job isn't to just make sure you obey your court sentence. I am also here to try and make sure you get the help you need to make sure you are never back here again. So, I think I will speak to your mother now. I assume that is her in the waiting room?"

"Yes."

A few minutes later, a confused and very anxious Claire appeared in the doorway of Sophie's small office.

"Please sit down, Mrs Airesdale," she said. "Jordan and I have just been discussing his progress and I am very pleased so far, but I have a few questions for you."

"Okay," she replied, nervously. "Ask away."

"First, let me say that it looks like you are doing a wonderful job in trying circumstances. I see a lot of parents who really struggle with a son or daughter on probation or parole. You seem to be doing very well."

Claire relaxed visibly.

"I notice that Jordan is in nappies and I wanted to ask if there is anything we need to know about it. I know he wets the bed and so that makes sense for nights, but is daytime for need or for discipline?"

Claire swallowed. Her nervousness was back again. "It's a bit of both. I made him wear them for discipline, but I found out he really needs them and so he is still in them."

"That's fine Claire, I just wanted to know if there was anything that you needed help with in that regard, like doctors' appointments or the like."

"No, she's... he's fine for now, thanks."

"Good to hear. I also discovered that you are smacking him, and I assume that is a regular thing?"

Claire threw a glance a Caitlyn, wondering what she had said to Sophie.

"I'm not criticising, you," Sophie quickly explained. "Frankly, if more parents spanked their teenagers, I'd have a whole lot less work to do."

"I spank him when he is disobedient or rude or angry."

"Well done."

Mother and daughter were stunned at Sophie's reaction. Spanking was very much out of fashion and even more so on your teenage son.

"Now, I do need to ask you about his earrings. He told me about the earrings you and your daughter bought them and they are very obviously... shall I say... feminine?"

"I suppose so," Claire responded cautiously.

"That's okay. I was just asking if Jordan wears girls' clothing at home and whether or not it would be preferable for him to wear them here. He clearly looks uncomfortable in trousers."

Sophie had seen it all in her ten years as a corrections officer. A teenage boy in nappies was a bit rare, although not unknown, but a teenage boy in girls' clothes was relatively common.

"Caitlyn?" Claire asked, speaking to her son/daughter.

She nodded. She didn't want to talk about it herself.

"Jordan has become Caitlyn in the last month. He feels more comfortable as a girl. He has been wearing his sister's clothes at home and he has his own girl's nightwear."

"Okay! I will write down Caitlyn as her name now and thank you for being honest. And in future, she can come here dressed the way she really is."

"Thank you," stammered Caitlyn, trying hard not to cry.

"Claire, does she have enough clothes of her own?"

"Around the home, she can do with what she has, but she can't really come here in her sister's clothes as they fit fairly well, but my other daughter wears short skirts and they... er..."

"Reveal Caitlyn's nappy?" Sophie offered.

"Yes exactly."

"Hmmm," said Sophie, thinking. "I can't promise anything, but I will ask my manager if Caitlyn could be permitted a three-hour shopping trip to buy girls' clothes that fit her. How would that be?"

"That would be wonderful, thank you," said Claire. "I was thinking about buying online, but I think for her first time, she needs to try things on properly."

"I agree and by the look of her hair, she is growing it, so in a month or two we might need to arrange a trip to the hairstylist."

"I was hoping to get someone willing to come to the house and do it, but that would be great if we can."

"I have an older son still in nappies, so I instantly recognised the shape of Caitlyn's trousers the first time she was here. I wasn't prying. I just could tell, and most other people wouldn't."

"Thanks for understanding."

"Next time Caitlyn, I hope to see those pretty earrings you told me about and see how pretty you are. See you in a month."

Surprise Visit

It was a good day when the children's swing set arrived. Caitlyn sat inside impatiently and watched from the window as the deliverymen set up the two-seater swing, a slip-and-slide and a large plastic shell which they filled with beach sand. The moment their van left through the front doors, she was outside, sliding down the slide and swinging on the swings.

She smiled and occasionally laughed for over two hours before Claire finally called her in for a much-delayed nappy change.

But the play equipment wasn't all that changed around the house. Bit by bit, the two women added new items to the nursery. A new soft toy, an extra doll, a baby's toy or a colouring-in book. Not wanting to overwhelm Caitlyn or to push too far too soon, the nursery became more and more of a playroom for the young girl.

Most days, Caitlyn would spend up to four hours in the nursery, playing with toys, building with Legos, drawing with pencils or cuddling a new doll. Jenny the teddy bear and she were inseparable. They slept together, played on the swings together, went for walks in the garden together and when she ate, Jenny sat on an empty chair at the table. From time to time, Claire would hear Caitlyn talking to her teddy bear like the friend she was becoming.

Her selection of baby clothes continued to grow, without making a big deal about it. In the morning, Claire might dress her in a new baby romper or a pretty new dress with a princess or an animal on it. As the nights got colder, pyjamas made way for footed sleepers and knitted baby bonnets. And the dummy was rarely out of her mouth.

It was 9 am one morning about two weeks after the last Parole Officer meeting that the front door rang. It was Sophie.

"Good morning, Claire," she said cheerfully, as the front door was opened. "I am just making a surprise visit to make sure Caitlyn is at home."

Claire had been fearing this day. She had always known that surprise visits would be happening but hoped she would be able to get her daughter ready for visitors. It would clearly not be happening that day.

"Come on in, take a seat," she stalled, trying to work out how to get Caitlyn ready to see a surprise visitor.

"No, that is fine. It should only take a few minutes. I only need to see her and make sure she is fine or actually, just still here."

Sensing that there was no way to avoid it, Claire told her that Caitlyn was in the nursery.

"She is just down the hall in an old nursery where she likes to play with toys."

Sophie threw an inscrutable look at Claire. The mention of toys obviously surprised her, but not completely.

As the two women stood wordlessly in the doorway of the nursery, Caitlyn played on the floor with some Legos, a collection of coloured pencils and a book scattered nearby. She was in a very pretty white and blue dress, a white bonnet and a yellow dummy in her mouth.

"This is how she likes to play," Claire explained quietly, hoping it would make sense.

"She looks adorable," Sophie whispered. "I thought there was more going on with her than just wearing nappies."

"Please don't tell anyone," Claire asked. "Caitlyn is just rediscovering herself and I don't want anyone interfering with her development."

Without answering, Sophie walked into the room and sat cross-legged in front of Caitlyn.

"Good morning, Caitlyn," she said. "What are you building?"

Caitlyn immediately recognised her Parole Officer, but instead of reacting, simply spat her dummy out and answered, "I'm building a house."

"That's lovely," she replied. "Do you like building houses a lot or any other things?"

"I build cars and towers and planes."

"Can you show me your other toys?"

While Claire watched in astonishment, Caitlyn took Sophie around the nursery and pointed out every one of the toys, teddies,

and dolls in the room. She showed her the new infant-age plastic toy she had gotten only the day before. And everywhere she went, Jenny went with her, tucked under her arm.

"And who is this, Caitlyn?" Sophie asked, pointing to the teddy bear that she was hugging with one arm.

"Jenny. She's my best friend."

"I see. Does Jenny sleep with you?"

Caitlyn nodded.

"I had a teddy bear when I was growing up too. His name was Benny. Can you tell me what animal is on your dress?"

Caitlyn looked down at the dress and said, "It's a hippo."

"That's right, Caitlyn. It's a hippo. Now you keep playing and your mummy and I will have a talk. It's lovely to speak with you again."

She put her dummy back in her mouth and went back to playing. Sophie and Claire walked out of the room.

"That was incredible," said Sophie, out of earshot of the nursery. "Right from the first time I met her, I could tell something was going on, but I couldn't work it out. When you told me that Jordan was actually a girl, I thought I knew what it was, but now… now, the nappies make a lot more sense."

Claire and Sophie sat down in the living room.

"I've been trying to manage her and get her straightened out and did what I thought was best."

"Please Claire," Sophie stated, holding up her hands. "I am not criticising you at all. I can see you are doing a wonderful job getting Caitlyn in line."

"I just had to put her in nappies again for my own sanity. The wet beds were just too much."

"She certainly looks very much like a girl, doesn't she?" Sophie commented.

"She sure does. It's surprised me just how feminine she looks if you dress her up properly."

"That is a gorgeous dress she is wearing and the colours really suit her. And I saw the change table. You are obviously serious about her being in nappies."

Claire began to relax as she realised that Sophie was not going to somehow have her arrested for babying her son. On the contrary, she seemed quite amenable to the idea.

"Jordan was a problem child for many years before he got in trouble with the police. He was unsettled and angry and he started stealing panties early on and in the end, we got him his own. It helped, but the anger was still there, and I lost control of him after his father died. That's when his bedwetting started up again."

"She doesn't look angry now."

"She isn't. She is very calm and happy being a girl," Claire sighed. "It has been astonishing."

"But it is more than being a girl, isn't it?" observed Sophie.

"She is more like a baby girl nowadays," admitted Claire. "Not all the time though. Caitlyn is still often a teenage girl and wants to put on makeup and skirts, but most of the time, she is like what you saw just now."

"I won't write anything down about this, so don't worry. My only job was to drop in unannounced this morning to make sure she was here – and she was."

"Thanks, Sophie, I appreciate it."

"But when she comes for her next appointment, she will still need to dress like an adult. She can't have a dummy or anything like that."

"I understand," she said and then laughed. "She has a dummy everywhere now! She doesn't go anywhere without one!"

Sophie leaned back in her chair, obviously in thought. "I actually know what that's like to some degree. I have a seven-year-old boy who still takes a dummy to bed. And he is still in nappies as well."

"Oh, okay," Claire said. She had no idea how to respond to what she had heard.

"I don't imagine he will be out of nappies any time soon, so in some respects, we are in a similar situation. Looking at Caitlyn, I don't see her getting out of nappies either."

"My daughter and I have both understood that Caitlyn might be in nappies forever. The shock of her arrest really pushed the wetting hard and that's why I got the change table, so it is easier on me."

"I see. Well, it is time for me to get going," exclaimed Sophie, standing up to leave. "I will leave you two alone and see her in two weeks' time!"

"Thanks for dropping in," said Claire. "I really appreciated the chat. I can't really talk to anyone else about this."

Sophie threw her head back and laughed. "This is the very first time anyone has ever thanked me for a surprise probation visit! You've made my day!"

Two weeks later, the big day came about for Caitlyn's first appearance outside the family home and everyone was nervous.

Her legs and armpits were freshly shaved. Connie had redone her nails the night before and Claire had taken the time to give her an early morning bath, washing her hair and ensuring she was

completely clean and fresh with no smell of wetness about her. A light spray of perfume helped.

Claire had ordered her some breast inserts to go inside the borrowed bra and with a camisole and top, looked very feminine. The online-ordered longer skirt fit well and covered the bulk of her nappy and panties.

For the first time in her life, Caitlyn wore pantyhose and then tried on the shoes that Claire had bought for her. Claire was nervous about buying shoes for her when she couldn't try them on. And it wasn't as if she could look at her other shoes for guidance. The only other shoes she had were boy's shoes or the pair of pink Crocs.

The fit wasn't great with the black flat shoes, but they were good enough for the morning trip. Claire had briefly thought of getting her shoes with heels, but thought better of it, given that she had never worn any heels at all before. The time to stumble and trip was not her first time out as a woman and even more so as a woman wearing a nappy.

"Mummy, I'm scared!" said Caitlyn as she sat down in the chair for her makeup.

"I know, honey," Claire answered. "You will be fine."

"You look gorgeous," said Connie, as she clipped the gold and diamond earrings in her ears. "You look better than most other girls."

Caitlyn grinned at her and lifted her hands to hold her 'breasts'.

"I can't wait until I grow my own!" she said.

"I know sweetheart," said Claire. "When this is all over, you can go on complete hormone treatment and have your own breasts. Won't that be wonderful?"

"Hold still, Caitlyn," Connie asked. "I still need to do your makeup. When you get to be a big girl, you will need to learn to do this yourself."

They were all quiet for a few minutes. They all realised that Caitlyn was a long way from being a 'big girl' yet. She had never changed her own nappy. She didn't dress herself and still had to ask permission for everything. Her idea of a fun morning was playing with all her toys. Doing her own makeup seemed as far away as flying cars.

But everyone was happy, nonetheless. Caitlyn, formerly Jordan, was now a very happy and contented little child. There was less anger and disobedience. The paddle had been unused for nearly two weeks – a record to date. But it was the sense of peace that made all the difference. Jordan was never at peace. Caitlyn was far happier and peaceful and baby Caitlyn was the happiest of them all.

Finally, the makeover was finished, and the two women stood back to inspect the results of their work.

Caitlyn was stunningly beautiful.

"Honey, you look lovely!" said her mother.

"Damn girl, you look prettier than me!" said Connie, handing out the ultimate compliment.

Caitlyn just grinned.

"Now, whatever you do, don't use your dummy or you'll spoil the lipstick, okay!"

It was finally time to leave home for the first time in a month and the first time ever as Caitlyn. It was the dreaded monthly Parole Officer meeting.

"Caitlyn Airesdale!" shouted the still disinterested receptionist as mother and daughter sat in the waiting room. Several young men in

The making of a baby

the room had eyed her up and down. It was probably a compliment, but in a Department of Corrections office, it felt quite creepy.

Caitlyn stood up and smoothed her skirt as she had been instructed and walked nervously down the corridor to Sophie's office.

"Come in and sit down, Caitlyn," said Sophie. "But first things first, are you wearing those earrings you promised to show me last time?"

Caitlyn pulled back her lengthening hair to reveal the earrings Connie had given her.

"Very pretty and they suit you very well. Now, do you remember me visiting you a couple of weeks ago?"

"Yes," she replied, putting her head down in embarrassment.

"There is no need to look like that, Caitlyn. You have nothing to be embarrassed about. My job is to make sure you stay in your house as the court ordered. How you dress when at home is none of my business."

"I like playing with toys," she explained.

"I could see that." Then Sophie went over to the filing cabinet in the corner of her office. There was a brown teddy bear sitting on top of it. "Would you like to hold one of my son's teddy bears while you are here?"

Caitlyn nodded.

"He has a lot of soft toys and I asked him if I could take Andie into work to keep me company."

She handed Andie to Caitlyn and she immediately hugged him like a long-lost friend.

"I thought you two might be friends," she commented, watching the interaction.

Over the next twenty minutes, Sophie talked with Caitlyn about her detention and all the usual questions.

"There is one thing I need to tell you and that is that my supervisor has approved a three-hour shopping trip for you and your mother to buy you your own suitable clothes and one shorter trip in two months' time to get your hair styled."

"Thank you, Sophie," Caitlyn replied. "It will be good to get out."

"I am sure it will be. I will speak to your mother about the details, as she will be the responsible adult with you. She will have to tell me where and when she is going and to ensure you are back home before the three hours is up."

"Mummy looks after me a lot," baby Caitlyn replied.

Sophie looked at the girl in her office and briefly saw the face of the toddler she had seen during her surprise visit. And then, just as quickly, the toddler was gone and the teenage girl was back.

"Yes, your mum is doing a good job with you and I hope you really appreciate that. Now if you give Andie back to me, you can go now and next time, I hope to see you in all your own clothes and not your sister's!"

Nursery

"When you have your boy finally settled into the toddler stage of behaviour, then is the time to move to the next step. You have been gradually taking away his independence and replacing it with a deep reliance on you for everything. You should already be responsible for all his nappy changes, choosing his clothes and dressing him, determining bed and nap times and circumscribing his daily activities. Now is the time to introduce babyish feeding. And the perfect start to that is the feeding bottle.

The making of a baby

Your boy is already addicted to his dummy, so he is already prepared for the sucking action of the bottle. The best time to introduce this is just before bed or a nap. The soporific effect of the warm bottle will make it easier to introduce.

For starters..."

Claire closed the book and sat back in her chair. She had read the passage on bottle-feeding a dozen times before and had often gotten the bottle out ready to go ahead but had stopped and put it back in the cupboard.

"Bottle-feeding is not a toddler activity as such; it is a baby one. Infants have formula bottles and once your boy is drinking from a bottle, he is officially an infant and all of the other infant activities and objects now come into play. You are ready to arrive at your destination – infancy."

Claire could recite that paragraph from memory. The last few weeks had been wonderful. Caitlyn had been happy and relaxed, but even as she watched her from a distance, she could tell that the job was not yet complete. She went to the kitchen and for the twentieth time, retrieved the glass baby bottle from the cupboard along with the opened, but unused, can of baby formula.

"Finally going to feed her?" asked Connie, who had walked in behind her unannounced.

"I think it is time now," she replied, as the hot water ran in the kitchen sink.

Caitlyn was already in bed after her bath and had been given half an hour of playtime before lights out. Nervously, Claire made up the single bottle of formula and then walked into Caitlyn's bedroom.

116

"Baby girl," she announced. "It is bedtime now, but before you go to sleep, I think you might like a special drink."

Caitlyn looked at the bottle and smiled.

"Now lie down and let's take your dummy out."

Caitlyn slipped down the bed and curled up as Claire removed the girl's dummy. She carefully placed the teat at her mouth and just as the book promised, greedily sucked at it, drawing in the warm formula into her tummy.

Connie came in and watched the amazing scene as Caitlyn drank the bottle down with eyes closed and slow steady breathing. When the bottle was finally emptied, Claire carefully pulled the teat out and quickly replaced it with her dummy. Her sucking barely missed a beat. And as they sat there quietly, Baby Caitlyn fell asleep and they quietly left the room, shutting the door behind them.

"It's time now, mum," said Connie.

"I know," her mother replied, knowingly.

When 7 am arrived the next morning, Claire came into Caitlyn's room to find her lying down awake and cuddling Jenny. But something else was in the room. It was the smell of a dirty nappy. It was Caitlyn's first accidental dirty nappy and had apparently occurred as she had slept.

"The first accidental dirty nappy is a powerful statement that your boy has finally arrived at infancy. When this first happens, you may be tempted to complain or to say something negative. The important thing is to say and do nothing at all. Make out as if it is the most normal thing in the world for your baby to dirty his nappy, awake or asleep because from now on... it is!

Congratulations on your new infant!"

Claire instantly recalled that paragraph from the book. And so, she ignored the dirty nappy.

"Good morning, baby," she said. "Would my little girl like a bottle?"

"Yes, Mumma," said the littlest girl yet.

"Stay in bed and I will get you one."

As she prepared her bottle, she recalled the word 'Mumma'.

"She is speaking much younger now. Was it the bottle?" she thought.

As she put the teat to her lips, she once again drank strongly and soon emptied it.

"Another one, baby?" Claire asked.

"Yes, Mumma, Mumma."

The second bottle went down much as the first one did. Connie briefly entered the room to see what was going on and quickly left, once she smelt the atmosphere.

"I think my little girl has a dirty nappy, doesn't she?" Claire exclaimed, smiling and poking her girl.

Caitlyn just giggled and laughed.

"I think a bath is called for, little girl. Let me go and get it started. Don't get up please!"

As she filled the bath, Connie came in and spoke to her.

"I see the bottle had quite the effect!" she smirked. "I could smell the result in the hallway!"

"It was always going to happen, so now it has, we just have to deal with it."

"*You* can deal with it, not me. I don't mind changing Caitlyn's wet nappies all that much, but her dirty ones are all yours!"

"I know and I guess that's fair. By the way, the rest of the furniture is coming today."

"I can't wait to see that! She is going to be *so* surprised."

Claire undressed Caitlyn carefully in the bathroom and her nappy was a disastrous brown mess. Her plastic pants had only just managed to keep her sleeper and sheets clean. Even as she wiped her up as best she could, she was instantly reminded of doing similar chores with Jordan as a baby of just twelve months of age and barely walking. The biggest difference was not her size, but rather her obvious femininity. It felt as if nothing else had changed. She was wiping clean a baby girl.

Connie had ordered some hormones for Caitlyn online and already, her breasts had begun to swell ever so slightly. As she sat in the bath, Claire could imagine she was seeing a twelve-month-old girl and not the boy that actually sat there.

She let her play in the bath for fifteen minutes before grabbing the soap and completing the task properly. That morning, Caitlyn was as young as she had ever seen her. 'Mumma' was proof that she was descending from toddler age into infancy. She was not even close to doing her personal hygiene properly and even less so after a massive nappy blowout.

With two bottles of formula in her belly, breakfast was no more than a couple of pieces of toast and jam and then it was off to play on the swings outside. It was a surprisingly warm and clear day and with tights, a long-sleeve baby dress and a bonnet, she was ready to play on the equipment and did so until lunchtime.

"Time for some bottles, Caitlyn!" Claire exclaimed, emerging from the kitchen with a tray carrying three piping hot bottles of formula. "But first, a bib for you. You make quite a mess with a bottle."

Just like any other baby, Caitlyn dribbled when bottle feeding.

"Now come and lie on the couch and put your head in my lap. There you go."

119

The making of a baby

As asked, the little girl laid down and put her head in her mother's lap and locked eyes with her. Taking out her dummy, Claire inserted the teat in Caitlyn's mouth and watched her greedily drink the first bottle.

"Time for another one!" Claire exclaimed. "My little baby girl was hungry, wasn't she?"

The time for pretence had passed. Caitlyn was a baby girl and there was no point denying it anymore. During moments of the day, she was the older teenager, but still a girl. But those moments were rarer and in fact, teenage Caitlyn had not been sighted for days. And now, toddler Caitlyn was making way for baby Caitlyn.

If not for the book that was directing her and explaining what was happening, Claire would have been totally lost. It had flabbergasted her almost a year earlier to discover that not only did some mothers regress their sons to babies to save them from themselves, but many of them were also babies inside anyhow and all they were doing was giving the baby inside a chance to come out. *Saving my Son* was the book that was now literally saving *her* son, except that her son was now her *daughter*. That was an additional aspect she was having to navigate on her own.

The three bottles were quickly drunk and after wiping her face, Caitlyn sat down at the table for a sandwich. Normally, there would be four sandwiches, but with three bottles in her tummy, she struggled to eat just one. And then she yawned.

It was time for the midday nap, now a part of her everyday ritual. She yawned on the change table as Claire changed her very wet nappy and then placed her in bed for her usual two-hour nap.

Claire was still astounded that baby Caitlyn could sleep ten hours at night and still need a two-hour nap at midday and some days, also need a short late afternoon nap if she had played a lot outside.

She was asleep only ten minutes when the truck arrived with a very special delivery.

The making of a baby

The two men – the same ones that had delivered the change table – took the panels to the nursery and in the middle of the large room assembled…

Her cot.

The single bed sized adult cot was carefully painted in pink and white, matching the change table and the colours of the nursery. Once it was assembled, the men carried in an oversized wooden playpen and placed it at one end of the nursery. And just before they left, they delivered a full-sized highchair which they placed in the dining room, replacing Caitlyn's regular chair.

All the furniture had been ordered two months before and awaiting delivery once the time was right and Caitlyn was ready for them. Now that her daughter had entered the infant phase of the program, a cot, highchair, and playpen were appropriate and essential.

While the baby slept, Claire prepared the nursery with all the other items she had carefully bought and collected over the months and hidden in her room.

She installed a baby mobile of small animals over the cot and put nursery print sheets and a princess quilt on the mattress, along with baby bumpers for the sides. She filled one end of the cot with soft toys and added a Fisher-Price play centre to one side to entertain her when she awoke early.

A collection of new toys, including a number of dolls, filled the shelves that had been empty for so long. The wardrobe already contained all of Caitlyn's baby clothes, but Claire opened up a box that contained three pairs of exquisite knitted baby booties and mittens in pink and white – all in Caitlyn's size. Only infants wore booties, not toddlers. She placed them in the drawer with her growing collection of bonnets.

With a few toys in the playpen, the nursery was now officially complete and Caitlyn's new permanent place. The last thing to do was

to peel back the double-sided tape and attach the decorative nameplate to the nursery door.

It simply said: **"Caitlyn's Nursery"**

Baby Caitlyn

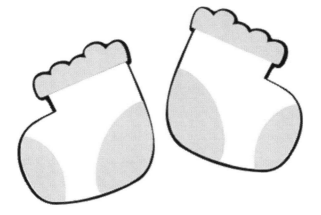

Connie raced to the Nursery the moment she arrived home that afternoon.

"Mum!" she exclaimed! "It looks fantastic!"

Connie lifted the side of the cot and then dropped it again. She checked out all the new toys and dolls and was doubly excited.

"I love the mobile, mum! You've really done a great job in here." Then she turned to the baby girl sitting in the far corner of the playpen holding some blocks. "Caitlyn, do you like your new cot?"

"Connie!" she exclaimed in her babyish voice. Then she crawled over to the entrance to the playpen and grinned.

"Looks like someone is loving her new nursery, aren't you!"

Caitlyn held her arms up in the air.

"Mum," said Connie warily. "What is she doing? I can't pick her up!"

Claire laughed. "She is asking you to get her out of the playpen. She has been doing that in the bath for weeks and the same to get out of bed. It's how she tells me she wants to get out."

Connie lifted the latch on the playpen and instead of walking out, Caitlyn crawled on all fours over to her new cot.

"Mum?" whispered Connie. "Why is she crawling?"

"She started crawling as soon as she saw the new cot and nursery. She's been on the floor ever since."

Claire lowered the side of the cot and Caitlyn climbed in. She then lifted the side again and the baby just sat and grinned.

"I think someone loves her new cot!" exclaimed Connie. "Does baby Caitlyn love her cot?"

"Yup... Connie," she lisped.

"Did you see her new booties?" asked Claire with a huge smile. "Don't they look gorgeous?"

Connie reached in and took hold of Caitlyn's foot and the pink bootie around it.

"They look amazing, mum. I didn't know you had them."

"I bought them online a few weeks ago. Now she has started crawling, booties make more sense than ever."

"I guess so. She really has become a baby, hasn't she?"

The irony of the conversation was perhaps that Claire and Connie were discussing Caitlyn's newly arrived full infancy in front of

her as if she could not understand what they were saying. The infant *could* understand, but when a rattle and a teddy bear were in the vicinity, as they were in the cot, she was too engrossed to listen or take any notice.

"It's nearly dinner time and so Caitlyn needs to have two bottles first. Would you be able to feed her for me?"

Connie swallowed hard. She knew this was coming and like everything else so far, she knew she could do it. And would do it. But she was still drawing the line at dirty nappies.

"Caitlyn, you need to have your bottles, sweetie," she said. "Let me get you out of the cot first."

Connie lowered the side of the cot and held Caitlyn's hand as she stepped out.

"Off we go to the dining room, so you can have your lovely bottles!"

"Connie... Connie..." It was a child's voice.

As soon as Connie took a step away from the cot, Caitlyn went back to all fours and began to crawl along the thickly carpeted floor towards the door. Connie walked slowly as the crawling infant reached the lush hallway runner and continued her way along the hall until she reached the dining room.

Connie sat on the couch and Caitlyn crawled up and placed her head on the woman's lap, just as she did with her mother.

"She needs a bib first and here are her three bottles," Claire explained. "I think she is very hungry now."

For the first time ever, Connie took the teat of the warm bottle and placed it in the mouth of her sister and looked on amazed as the little girl latched on and fed just like an infant.

"She's just like a baby, isn't she?" commented Claire, looking on with a smile. "She has been like this all day. I've not seen her be anything else other than a baby."

"So, it's finally happened then?" asked Connie.

"I think so. Caitlyn is finally a baby."

"You know, I never thought you could do it," Connie sighed. "I never thought that book made any sense before."

Connie looked down at the form of her now-baby sister, as she started on her second bottle.

"But she just looks and acts like a baby completely. Is that what Jordan's problem was all along? That he was just a baby girl still?"

"I don't know for sure. I do know that she is clearly a girl and that really messed her around. Perhaps being a baby again gives her the chance to be what she always wanted to be, but never was."

"Did you know she was a girl when she was little?"

"No, not really. I knew something was a little 'off', but I didn't know what. And her bedwetting just threw me off and I thought *that* was the problem. I didn't realise it was just a symptom."

Connie began the third bottle.

"So, does she stay a baby forever or what?"

"That's the big question and we don't know. Some girls like her will grow right back into young women. Some stay infants forever and others, they grow up as adult babies with both big and little in them."

"And Caitlyn?"

"Too soon to say, I'm afraid. But I do know the chances of toilet training are remote. She will be in nappies forever, that's for sure."

"When her home detention is over, where can she go to anyhow? A playground? Day Care?"

Claire smiled. "She'd probably love a playground. She adores the swings here and plays on them for hours. Sadly, I don't think Day Care is an option!"

The third bottle was finally finished.

The making of a baby

"Caitlyn, it's time to try out your new highchair!"

The little girl surprisingly walked the short distance to the dining room where her sparkling new highchair sat. She climbed up into it and Claire quickly adjusted and clipped the restraining straps. She then took the tray and clicked it into place. It was now time for her first dinner as a baby. Feeding herself was now as much a thing of the past as was dressing and bathing. From now on, she would need to be fed.

Claire cut up her meat and vegetables and spoon-fed her the entire meal. It was a messy affair and the bib did good service. Mashed potato ended up smeared over her face. But the entire time, Caitlyn smiled and said little more than baby babbles.

"You can play on the floor here for ten minutes, baby, and then it is bedtime for you."

Instinctively, Connie looked up at the clock. It said 6:50 pm.

"I'm changing her bedtime to seven pm now," Claire explained. "She is already tired and yawning. Nine pm is much too late for a baby girl."

Ten minutes later, both women took the increasingly tired baby girl down to the nursery for her first night sleeping in the cot. Connie volunteered – a first – to change her nappy for bed, while Claire found a suitable footed sleeper and matching bonnet.

"Give Connie a kiss and hug goodnight, please," said Claire.

Caitlyn hugged her older sister tight and gave her a kiss on the cheek. Connie kissed her back on the forehead.

"Have a good sleep little girl!" she said.

"Give mummy a hug and kiss too, sweetheart," Claire asked, and the little girl did just that, giving her mother a big kiss and cuddle. "Up into the cot now."

Baby Caitlyn laid back in the cot while her mother tucked her in and gave her Jenny and one of her dolls to sleep with. Three more teddy bears sat at the end of the cot. Then she leaned over and kissed the yawning infant one more time on the forehead.

"Mumma, Mumma, Mumma," she repeated.

Connie leant over and also kissed her again.

"Connie... Connie..."

Connie had tears in her eyes as she turned away and held her mother tight.

"She's just a baby, mum," she whispered, tears beginning to flow. "She's just a baby."

"I know, hun," she replied, as they continued to embrace. "She has been like this all day."

"I've never seen her this happy. Never in her entire life!"

Grasping Connie's hand, her mother led her out and to the living room where both women began to weep silently.

"Jordan had so much anger and so much frustration," Claire said. "He punched a hole in his wall, he was so angry."

"And now he is a baby girl sleeping in a cot!"

Claire turned on the baby monitor and together they watched the extraordinary vision.

The room was dimly lit with just a Princess nightlight keeping the darkness at bay. The mobile spun slowly above her head, with the quiet sound of the nursery rhyme barely audible.

In the quietness, they could hear Caitlyn making sounds. She was saying 'Mumma' and 'Bubba' and 'Connie' and one other word that sounded like 'jenny'. The rest of it was baby-like sounds.

Five minutes later, the babbling stopped, her eyes closed, and she was asleep. It was the first night in her cot and her new nursery. It was also her first night as a full infant girl.

Shopping with Caitlyn

Four days later, the doorbell rang and once again, Sophie was there to check up on Caitlyn.

"Sorry to barge in," she explained. "But you know the drill. Can I see Caitlyn please?"

"I just put her down for her midday nap," she explained. "She is well asleep by now."

"Is she still wearing baby clothes like she was last time?" Sophie asked. "She looked so pretty."

"Why don't you come and take a look," Claire responded. "But do you really need to talk to her?"

"Technically yes, but as long as she is here, my report will be fine. But I'd like to see her just the same."

Claire quietly opened the door to 'Caitlyn's Nursery'. She already knew she was asleep as she had seen her on the baby monitor.

"She's in a cot now?" Sophie asked.

"Just for a few days now, but she sleeps better in one and it is, shall we say…"

"More appropriate?" suggested Sophie.

"Exactly. Far more suited to her."

"Well I am obviously happy she is here, but it does perhaps cause a potential problem for her next appointment with me next week."

"I know," replied Claire, her brow furrowed. "I am not sure how to handle it."

"From the little I understand, Caitlyn is both a teenage girl and baby girl, right?"

"Yes, I think so, more or less."

"She quite simply can't come to the office as a baby girl. She has to come as a teenage girl. Do you think you can get her to do that?"

"To be honest, I don't know. She is loving being a baby girl and I haven't tried to get her to be a teenage girl for a week or so."

"You need to work it out because her appointment is ten days away. But I did want to tell you that she has been approved for a shopping trip and I volunteered to accompany you and her. I didn't

want any of the other buffoons doing it and making it harder than it already is."

"When can we do it? I am fairly flexible, obviously."

"How about this Friday at 10 am and you have three hours. If you want, I can pick you two up and take you into the city. That way, if you are a little longer, no one will give you trouble for it, if you had just gone alone. It's also a bit of a safe trial run to being in public as a girl."

Friday at 10 am came quickly.

Connie and her mother had done their very best to make Caitlyn as pretty and feminine as possible and she was reasonably adult as well. She was communicating as a teenager, if a little young still. By the time Sophie picked them both up, Caitlyn was coping pretty well.

"It must still be a bit odd to be going outside your home like this," said Sophie, as they drove down the freeway toward the city.

"It's only the second time I've been outside dressed as a girl and it's a bit freaky, especially going shopping."

"Are you nervous?"

"After going to court three months ago, this is definitely a lot easier," she joked. "But I've still never gone shopping as a girl before, so I am a bit freaked someone will see me."

"Well, you have two experienced women to help you out. The Department is not interested in penalising you for being transgender and we are supposed to help out. The nappy thing though is not

something we talk about. But you aren't the first person I've dealt with wearing nappies if it is any consolation."

"Really?" asked Claire. "What happened?"

"A while back, I had a 35-year-old man on probation and he was wearing nappies all the time and made no big deal about it."

"I have to wear nappies now," offered Caitlyn. "I just find it too hard now to stay dry."

"I do understand, Caitlyn," replied Sophie. "My job today is to help you get girl's clothes and set you up to be better prepared for life after your detention is over. We are not all hard-arses, you know!"

"I appreciate that. I thought it was going to be really horrible, but so far, it has been okay. Mummy even bought me some swings to play on!"

Using the word 'mummy' in such an infantile manner ended the conversation and the car stayed silent until they drove into the shopping centre carpark. No one was sure how to deal with the infant and hoped she would disappear and leave the teenager there.

Terrified of how she might react, Claire took hold of Caitlyn's hand and they walked to the first of several clothing stores. Normally a shopping trip like this would take half a day, but they only had three hours and that included travel time.

In double-quick time, Claire's credit card bought two new outfits, including two pairs of shoes, one of which had a small heel on them. Perhaps the most nerve-wracking moment came when they selected two new bras for her. Caitlyn's breasts had only just started to sprout and so she was soon going to need to wear a bra, baby clothes or not. So, Claire selected a training bra that she could wear right now, including under baby clothes and a full-size bra to wear with her breast inserts. If the training bra worked out, she would get more for her to wear as she grew.

"It's incredible how her breasts have grown so much in only a couple of months," she mused. "It won't be long before she will have a full set!"

With still a little time left on their allotted three hours, Claire took Caitlyn into a Jewellery shop and Sophie watched dumbfounded as Claire spent a small fortune on a beautiful gold, diamond and sapphire necklace and matching bracelet.

"That looks fabulous on you!" exclaimed Sophie, trying desperately to not sound jealous. "It really makes you look pretty."

On the ride home, Caitlyn was much happier and confident in her completely new outfit and jewellery. They arrived home a mere five minutes before the allotted three hours was up.

"Do you want to come in for a moment, Sophie?" asked Claire politely. "I should at least offer you some tea or coffee after all you've done for us today."

"That would be lovely, thank you."

"Caitlyn needs to change her nappy though, so do you mind for a few minutes?"

"Of course," she said. "Go and change her. It's not like I didn't know you are the one changing her nappies before now!"

Claire breathed a sigh of relief.

"I'm glad. I didn't want you to think I was doing anything weird or wrong."

Sophie chuckled. "I was changing my own brother's nappies until I left home and he was fifteen then, so no, I am quite okay with it. What needs to be done, needs to be done."

Claire quickly changed a nearly overflowing wet nappy in the nursery while Sophie patiently waited for them.

"You've done a remarkable job with Caitlyn, you know," Sophie remarked while drinking her tea.

"I thought Jordan was heading to jail and it was my last chance to do something to stop him going that direction."

"You were probably right and that's why I am pleased how it is turning out. Letting Jordan transition into Caitlyn is probably the key and of course, the baby thing that you do for her is helping as well."

Claire blushed.

"Don't be embarrassed. He wet the bed, so nappies were always going to come back and the day nappies seems like they were needed as well."

"They certainly are now!" Claire exclaimed. "He was wetting them constantly, only days after going back into them. I obviously mucked up his toilet training somewhere along the line."

"Don't be harsh on yourself. By the end of her home detention, you will have a happy and confident teenage girl ready to take on the world."

"While wearing nappies..."

"That's nothing. Nappies are no big deal nowadays."

"But you've seen her as a little girl," Claire replied. "It's more than just nappies now. It's a lot more complex. She's even moved into the nursery now."

"Would you mind if I saw the nursery again?"

Claire took her to the nursery where Caitlyn was sitting on the floor playing with toys, still in her new clothes.

"When did you get the cot?" Sophie exclaimed. "It looks beautiful."

"I had it made by the same people that made the change table. Caitlyn has only been sleeping in it for a bit over a week. And on that topic, she is late for her midday nap."

"Oh sorry, I should get going anyhow. I look forward to seeing you both at your next appointment."

The making of a baby

As soon as Sophie had left, Claire undressed the exhausted, now-baby Caitlyn, put her sleeper on and put her into the cot. She was too tired to even have her pre-nap bottle.

The remaining nine months of Caitlyn's detention passed reasonably quickly. Life soon developed a ritual and pattern that made it easier for everyone to manage and deal with.

Caitlyn changed from a midday nap to a shorter mid-morning nap and another mid-afternoon one as a single nap was proving too much for her. She transitioned into being largely bottle-fed with some soft baby foods three times a day with a bit of adult food added in.

Teenage Caitlyn was reserved for meetings with Sophie and occasionally, other times. For her part, Sophie dropped in unannounced at least once a month and usually saw the infant girl. Most of the time it felt like she dropped in for a chat and a chance to see the baby girl in her natural environment. Her job simply provided her with a good reason.

Connie took over a lot more of the care responsibilities including the occasional dirty nappy and particularly, bathing, where Caitlyn really needed help and monitoring. And every night at 7 am, Connie would put her to bed and read her a bedtime story. She dearly loved storytime and the two sisters developed a very strong, if unusual, relationship. It was the best part of the day for Connie.

Crawling became a common form of moving around, interspersed with some walking. By the end of detention, when not in teenager more, Caitlyn's speech was restricted to just a few real words and the rest, mostly just baby babble.

The making of a baby

In the warmer afternoons, Claire would set up the small playpen outside on the lawn with a few toys and would sometimes fall asleep under the sun, assured that her baby daughter was safe and could not get into trouble. Some days, home detention was an ironically idyllic life for mother and daughter.

Despite being in home detention, it was a wonderful time for Caitlyn as she developed her infancy and her femininity. The physical boundaries of her home were much larger than the emotional boundaries that had been hers growing up as a boy instead of a girl and as a teenager, instead of an infant.

The day came, however, when her detention was finally over. She could now leave the house without restriction.

After breakfast, Claire and Connie had intended to take a teenage Caitlyn out for a drive and into the city for lunch and perhaps a movie – a way to celebrate freedom, not just from detention, but from her ill-fated boy past. Baby Caitlyn however, refused to budge. She wasn't going anywhere as a teen girl. She was only going out as a baby and any attempt to change that led to crying and tantrums.

Working out an alternative plan, they dressed Baby Caitlyn in some appropriate play clothes and shoes and the inevitable dummy and drove a short distance to a large park.

Very nervously, the two women held Caitlyn's hand as they walked to the playground and watched as the little girl jumped on the swings and swung to her heart's content.

Up and down the slide she went and then back onto the swings once more. There was a small wooded area nearby and holding her hand, they walked through the trees and bushes. It was all new to Caitlyn. This was a girl who had been 'born' in home detention and had never really ventured out of the house. Those twelve-month old eyes had never seen a large park or so many trees. She was revelling in the experience of newness.

"It's a pity she can't go to many places like she is, isn't it!" exclaimed Connie, sadly. "My baby sister deserves everything any other child has."

Connie had grown very protective of her baby sister over the last year, even to the extent of changing dirty nappies and bathing her without complaint. She saw nothing masculine in her anymore, only a very infantile baby that occasionally rose to the age of a young teenager.

"I agree, Connie," sighed Claire, watching the baby holding dried leaves in her hands and crushing them. "There's not many places a girl like Caitlyn can go."

"Well, I am glad we have at least one other person who accepts her. I really like Sophie."

Claire laughed. "It's ironic isn't that the one person that accepts Caitlyn as a baby is her Parole Officer?"

"Yeah, it is a bit. I don't know how she could find other friends like her. I know there are adult babies and such, but Caitlyn is a bit different than most."

"I know. She is really just a baby and little else. I do love her like this though. Don't you?"

Her mother already knew that Connie loved her sister deeply and was fiercely protective of her.

"She is just so pretty!" exclaimed Connie. "I know she was once a boy, but unless you changed her nappy, you wouldn't know! And now her breasts are coming in, she is really quite sweet looking."

"Well it's getting on and you know we have that party this afternoon and Caitlyn needs to at least get her midday nap or she will be too tired and cranky to enjoy it."

"As parties go, it is a bit lame though, isn't it? Just us and Sophie and her husband?"

"We have to celebrate the end of her detention somehow and a small party is better than none at all."

As they walked through the playground, a middle-aged couple saw them and stared rather obviously. Caitlyn ignored them, concentrating instead on skipping, while still holding both her mother's and sister's hands.

A happier child could not be found anywhere.

Celebration

I t was four o'clock in the afternoon.

While Caitlyn slept, Connie used her creative flair and hung balloons and streamers around the house and other decorations around the backyard where the play equipment was.

"It might be a small party," she said aloud to no one at all. "But it's going to be a party, just the same!"

It was the ultimate 'coming out' party for Caitlyn. Not only was she 'coming out' of home detention, but she was also coming out as a girl and coming out as a baby. It was all a very big deal. So naturally, presents were required. And a cake.

After waking up, Claire went to town on Caitlyn's appearance. After a bath, she pinned her into brand new, fluffy terry nappies and equally brand new, frilly pink plastic pants with circular ruffles on the back and lace around the legs. Now that she was literally 'growing up', she put her in a pink and white lace padded bra to accentuate her now B-cup and still developing breasts. And on top, she had a pink and white baby dress with *Mummy's Baby* embroidered on it.

White bobby socks and Mary Jane shoes encouraged her to walk on her special day since crawling would mess up her pretty clothes. Her now very long hair had been styled in waves and the baby bonnet she wore looked adorable. Around her wrist was a new bracelet with the words *Baby Caitlyn* engraved on it – a gift from Connie several months earlier. And as always, a dummy was attached to her dress with a ribbon.

Caitlyn was the guest of honour and had to look the part.

It was 4:30 when their sole party guest arrived.

As the familiar SUV pulled up the driveway, they could see Sophie behind the wheel, but also two indistinct figures in the seat behind her.

Sophie grinned as she opened the back door of the vehicle and as Claire, Connie and Caitlyn approached, she introduced the first person.

"Ladies, this is baby Jerry, my husband."

A tall man stood out wearing a baby boy's romper and a bulging and rather obvious nappy. A blue dummy was in his mouth and a white baby bonnet was around his head.

The making of a baby

"Remember that seven-year-old boy I told you about?" Sophie exclaimed, still grinning. "Well, that was really baby Jerry. And he is in nappies all the time, just like Caitlyn!"

Then the other side of the car opened and out stepped a girl. But not just any girl. It was a baby girl.

"And this is baby Serena, a baby friend of Jerry's who wanted to come to the party as well."

Serena was quite simply, adorable. She was also wearing a pink dress and a pink bonnet and an equally bulging nappy and sucking on a dummy. She was hugging a doll.

Claire was stunned into wordlessness and so, Sophie stepped in.

"Jerry and Serena, meet baby Caitlyn. It is her party today and she is telling the world she is a baby girl!"

Baby Jerry stepped up and gave Caitlyn a big hug. "Happy birthday!"

Caitlyn looked surprised and confused as Serena walked up, took her dummy out and gave her a big kiss on the lips. "Happy birthday, Caitlyn!"

"Come around the back everyone," announced Claire. "The party is set up there."

Sidling up to Sophie, she exclaimed, "Why didn't you tell me you had an adult baby?"

"While Caitlyn was in detention it was inappropriate to talk to you about it, but as of two days ago... I am free to tell you everything. And I hope you didn't mind bringing Serena along as well."

"No, not at all," she stammered. "She is gorgeous, but is she a girl or a boy? I can't tell."

Sophie laughed. "Why does it matter? Just like Caitlyn, she is just a baby."

"Where did you meet her?"

"Jerry met her online and found she lives locally. She's twenty-two and lives alone and they hit it off and have been playmates for the last year. They are very good for each other. I am hoping the three of them might be good friends as well. Caitlyn is going to need some baby friends."

Claire was overwhelmed by the sight of three adult-sized babies skipping and holding hands as they went along the path at the side of the house towards the party at the rear.

Like every birthday party that has ever been held, there was more food than they could possibly consume, even with an extra guest. The three babies played on the swings and slide and laughed and talked as they ran around the garden.

Ever the observant one, Connie noticed that the three babies spoke very simply and often in little more than baby babble but somehow, were communicating perfectly with each other. Before being allowed to eat, Claire put a bib on Caitlyn and Sophie tied bibs on the other two.

Claire then stood up and asked everyone to be quiet. Connie held Caitlyn's hand to keep her still and in one place.

"Just over a year ago, my child and I began a journey together, a journey of discovery. My darling baby girl Caitlyn, began to emerge from the shadows where she has suffered for so long. It took her sister and me a long time to see what you see before you today – a baby girl who is beautiful, happy and wondrously loving.

"Today is a very special day for her. My daughter has not only come out of home detention, but she has also come out of being denied who she is. Caitlyn is a girl, not a boy. She also showed us all that she is more than just a girl. She is a *baby* girl, a baby that is everything any new mother could ever want.

"But today is even more special than that. It is more than just a *coming out*. Twelve months ago, to the day, my little girl first went back into nappies and in a very, very tiny way, that little baby girl was born that very moment."

Claire looked at Caitlyn with tears in her eyes. "Today is your very first birthday! Today, you are one year old! Happy birthday, Baby Caitlyn!"

The party immediately began to sing Happy Birthday to the smiling and laughing child, as Claire brought out her one-year-old birthday cake.

"And here are your presents!" announced Connie, as she came back out of the house with a handful of carefully wrapped gifts.

Like any other one year old, Caitlyn sat on the ground and opened all of her presents. Baby Jerry and Baby Serena also gave her a present and soon the ground was scattered with hastily torn wrapping paper. More toys, more clothes and more fun were just what the party needed.

As the three adults sat around and talked, the three babies played and laughed until the sunset. It was not unnoticed that Serena and Caitlyn held hands much of the time.

By 7:30, Caitlyn was yawning and rubbing her eyes and Claire declared that it was her bedtime. It was late already, but she couldn't stay up any longer

In the nursery, Sophie stood and watched, chatting amicably while Claire changed a wet nappy and dressed Caitlyn for bed. It had been a great day, but in retrospect, it had also been a great year.

As Caitlyn drifted off to sleep, both women bent over and kissed her.

Baby Caitlyn had been born on May 19th and one year later, was finally the infant girl she had always been inside.

She was finally home.

Epilogue

"When your ~~boy~~-girl finally arrives at infancy, several things might happen. ~~He~~ she may just stay there and be a baby forever or ~~he~~ she may bounce right back to ~~his~~ her teenage self and go on. Another possibility and the most likely is that ~~he~~ she will then begin to grow up slowly and naturally. ~~He~~ she will begin to mature and change and like any other child, develop and grow. How far or how fast ~~he~~ she goes is not possible to tell and largely up to you. But as your child grows up this second time you can mould ~~him~~ her to be the child you want. Nappies will be forever, as toilet training is what messed things up in the first place. This is the journey that can be wondrous and spectacular and deeply rewarding."

Claire put down the pen that she had used to cross out *him* and replace it with *her*. Even the cover of the book now said *Saving my ~~Son~~ Daughter*. The book had been remarkable, a template of the journey she had embarked on. But it had missed gender changes completely and so with a smile, Claire had selectively altered the text.

It had been two years now since Caitlyn's first birthday and true to the book, she had started to grow up some. The guests had just gone home from her third birthday party and she had enjoyed the company of some nine babies not dissimilar to herself. The nursery was quiet now and the mobile was the only sign of movement on the baby monitor.

Teenage Caitlyn had developed enough confidence to leave the house and get a job and while she was actually twenty-one years old, she looked and acted more like the eighteen-year-old she had been when she first appeared. Working as a receptionist in an office, none of her colleagues knew she was anything other than a well-mannered, capable and extremely attractive young woman. But at home, it was baby Caitlyn's safe place. From the moment she arrived back home, she was that three-year-old she had slowly grown into.

She was still in a cot and still in nappies, although at work, she wore discreet disposable ones. Bottles still fed her morning and night and Claire still changed her nappies. Connie had moved out but was still frequently back in the nursery changing nappies, feeding bottles or bathing the three-year-old. Her baby sister was too important to abandon.

There was also a second cot in the nursery now.

Caitlyn and Serena were now more than just friends. The term 'dating' didn't really apply to two baby girls that loved to play together, hold hands and kiss. That was far too mature a concept. They did, however, have sleepovers now and Claire had bought a second cot to accommodate her.

Claire smiled as she recalled the incident a week earlier. Still immensely shy, Serena had always changed her own nappy in private and both Claire and Caitlyn respected that. But that particular night as the girls got ready for bed and Claire had just finished changing Caitlyn, Serena nervously asked her to change her nappy for bed.

Thrilled to be finally trusted with such a responsibility, she placed her on the change table and unpinned and removed her soaking wet nappy. Then, for just an instant, she stopped and stared at Serena's vagina.

Claire realised that she had never even considered the possibility that Serena had been born a girl.

And then she finally realised the truth about the wonderful relationship between Baby Caitlyn and Baby Serena.

It simply didn't matter. They were just two baby girls who loved each other.

THE END

Now that you have read this book you might be interested in more of Michael's and Rosalie's books. Go to h https://abdiscovery.com.au/michael-and-rosalie-bent/ to find more of their work. You will also find our complete collection of AB fiction and non-fiction.

An AB Discovery Book

SAVING
MY
SON

*One woman's story of how she saved her son
from a life of violence and death by taking him
right back to the start - as a baby*

AMANDA MARSDEN

An AB Discovery Book

SAVING

MY

SON

DAUGHTER!

*One woman's story of how she saved her son
from a life of violence and death by taking him
right back to the start - as a baby*

AMANDA MARSDEN

CLAIRE AIRESDALE

Made in the USA
Middletown, DE
22 February 2023